A Soldier's Embrace

Stories by

NADINE GORDIMER

PENGUIN BOOKS

PENGUIN BOOKS

Published by the Penguin Group
Penguin Books Ltd, 27 Wrights Lane, London W8 5TZ, England
Penguin Books USA Inc., 375 Hudson Street, New York, New York 10014, USA
Penguin Books Australia Ltd, Ringwood, Victoria, Australia
Penguin Books Canada Ltd, 10 Alcorn Avenue, Toronto, Ontario, Canada M4V 3B2
Penguin Books (NZ) Ltd, 182–190 Wairau Road, Auckland 10, New Zealand

Penguin Books Ltd, Registered Offices: Harmondsworth, Middlesex, England

First published in the United States of America by
The Viking Press 1980
Published in the United States by
arrangement with Alfred A. Knopf, Inc.
Published in Penguin Books 1982
13 15 17 19 20 18 16 14 12

LIBRARY OF CONGRESS CATALOGING IN PUBLICATION DATA
Gordimer, Nadine.
A soldier's embrace.
I. Title.
PR9369.3.G6S6   1982   823   81-11975
ISBN 0 14 00.5925 3   AACR2

Printed in England by Clays Ltd, St Ives plc
Set in Plantin

"A Soldier's Embrace" and "A Lion on the Freeway" appeared originally in
Harper's; "Town and Country Lovers" in *The New Yorker* under the title
"City Lovers"; "Oral History" in *Playboy*.

PENGUIN BOOKS

A SOLDIER'S EMBRACE

Nadine Gordimer was born and lives in South Africa. She has written nine novels, including *A Guest of Honour*, which won the James Tait Black Prize; *The Conservationist*, which was co-winner of the Booker Prize in England; *Burger's Daughter*, *July's People* and most recently *A Sport of Nature*. Her short stories have been collected in eight volumes. Many of her books have been published in Penguin. Ms. Gordimer has also received the French international literary prize, the Grand Aigle d'Or and was awarded the Scottish Arts Council's Neil Gunn Fellowship for 1981. Her writings have appeared in many American magazines, including *The New Yorker*, *Harper's Atlantic Monthly*, and *The New York Review of Books*. Ms. Gordimer travels widely in Africa, Europe, and the United States.

Nadine Gordimer was awarded the 1991 Nobel Prize for Literature.

by the same author

novels
A GUEST OF HONOUR
THE LATE BOURGEOIS WORLD
OCCASION FOR LOVING
A WORLD OF STRANGERS
THE LYING DAYS
THE CONSERVATIONIST
BURGER'S DAUGHTER
JULY'S PEOPLE
A SPORT OF NATURE

short stories
LIVINGSTONE'S COMPANIONS
NOT FOR PUBLICATION
FRIDAY'S FOOTPRINT
SIX FEET IN THE COUNTRY
THE SOFT VOICE OF THE STREET
SELECTED STORIES
SOMETHING OUT THERE

CONTENTS

A Soldier's Embrace 7
A Lion on the Freeway 23
Siblings 29
Time Did 45
A Hunting Accident 55
For Dear Life 67
Town and Country Lovers *One* 73
Two 85
A Mad One 95
You Name It 105
The Termitary 113
The Need for Something Sweet 121
Oral History 133

For Paule Taramasco

A SOLDIER'S EMBRACE

The day the cease-fire was signed she was caught in a crowd. Peasant boys from Europe who had made up the colonial army and freedom fighters whose column had marched into town were staggering about together outside the barracks, not three blocks from her house in whose rooms, for ten years, she had heard the blurred parade-ground bellow of colonial troops being trained to kill and be killed.

The men weren't drunk. They linked and swayed across the street; because all that had come to a stop, everything *had* to come to a stop: they surrounded cars, bicycles, vans, nannies with children, women with loaves of bread or basins of mangoes on their heads, a road gang with picks and shovels, a Coca-Cola truck, an old man with a barrow who bought bottles and bones. They were grinning and laughing amazement. That it could be: there they were, bumping into each other's bodies in joy, looking into each other's rough faces, all eyes crescent-shaped, brimming greeting. The words were in languages not mutually comprehensible, but the cries were new, a whooping and crowing all understood. She was bumped and jostled and she let go, stopped trying to move in any self-determined direction. There were two soldiers in front of her, blocking her off by their clumsy embrace (how do you do it, how do you do what you've never done before) and the embrace opened like a door and took her in—a pink hand with bitten nails grasping her right arm, a black hand with a big-dialled watch and thong bracelet pulling at her left elbow. Their three heads collided gaily, musk of sweat and tang of strong sweet soap clapped a mask to her nose and mouth. They all gasped with delicious shock. They were saying things to each other. She put up an arm round each neck, the rough pile of an army haircut on one side, the soft negro hair on the other, and kissed them both on the cheek. The embrace broke. The crowd wove her away behind backs, arms, jogging heads; she was returned to and took up the will of her direction again—she was walking home from the post office, where she had just sent a telegram to relatives abroad: ALL CALM DON'T WORRY.

The lawyer came back early from his offices because the courts were not sitting although the official celebration holiday was not until next day. He described to his wife the rally before the Town Hall, which he had watched from the office-building balcony. One of the guerilla leaders (not the most important; he on whose head the biggest price had been laid would not venture so soon and deep into the territory so newly won) had spoken for two hours from the balcony of the Town Hall. 'Brilliant. Their jaws dropped. Brilliant. They've never heard anything on that level: precise, reasoned—none of them would ever have believed it possible, out of the bush. You should have seen de Poorteer's face. He'd like to be able to get up and open his mouth like that. And be listened to like that...' The Governor's handicap did not even bring the sympathy accorded to a stammer; he paused and gulped between words. The blacks had always used a portmanteau name for him that meant the-crane-who-is-trying-to-swallow-the-bullfrog.

One of the members of the black underground organization that could now come out in brass-band support of the freedom fighters had recognized the lawyer across from the official balcony and given him the freedom fighters' salute. The lawyer joked about it, miming, full of pride. 'You should have been there— should have seen him, up there in the official party. I told you— really—you ought to have come to town with me this morning.'

'And what did you do?' She wanted to assemble all details.

'Oh I gave the salute in return, chaps in the street saluted *me*... everybody was doing it. *It was marvellous*. And the police standing by; just to think, last month—only last week—you'd have been arrested.'

'Like thumbing your nose at them,' she said, smiling.

'Did anything go on around here?'

'Muchanga was afraid to go out all day. He wouldn't even run up to the post office for me!' Their servant had come to them

many years ago, from service in the house of her father, a colonial
official in the Treasury.

'But there was no excitement?'

She told him: 'The soldiers and some freedom fighters mingled
outside the barracks. I got caught for a minute or two. They were
dancing about; you couldn't get through. All very good-natured.
—Oh, I sent the cable.'

An accolade, one side a white cheek, the other a black. The
white one she kissed on the left cheek, the black one on the right
cheek, as if these were two sides of one face.

That vision, version, was like a poster; the sort of thing that was
soon peeling off dirty shopfronts and bus shelters while the months
of wrangling talks preliminary to the take-over by the black
government went by.

To begin with, the cheek was not white but pale or rather
sallow, the poor boy's pallor of winter in Europe (that draft must
have only just arrived and not yet seen service) with homesick
pimples sliced off by the discipline of an army razor. And the
cheek was not black but opaque peat-dark, waxed with sweat
round the plump contours of the nostril. As if she could return
to the moment again, she saw what she had not consciously noted:
there had been a narrow pink strip in the darkness near the ear,
the sort of tender stripe of healed flesh revealed when a scab is
nicked off a little before it is ripe. The scab must have come away
that morning: the young man picked at it in the troop carrier
or truck (whatever it was the freedom fighters had; the colony
had been told for years that they were supplied by the Chinese and
Russians indiscriminately) on the way to enter the capital in
triumph.

According to newspaper reports, the day would have ended for
the two young soldiers in drunkenness and whoring. She was,
apparently, not yet too old to belong to the soldier's embrace of all
that a land-mine in the bush might have exploded for ever. That
was one version of the incident. Another: the opportunity taken
by a woman not young enough to be clasped in the arms of the one

who (same newspaper, while the war was on, expressing the fears of the colonists for their women) would be expected to rape her.

She considered this version.

She had not kissed on the mouth, she had not sought anonymous lips and tongues in the licence of festival. Yet she had kissed. Watching herself again, she knew that. She had—god knows why —kissed them on either cheek, his left, his right. It was deliberate, if a swift impulse: she had distinctly made the move.

She did not tell what happened not because her husband would suspect licence in her, but because he would see her—born and brought up in the country as the daughter of an enlightened white colonial official, married to a white liberal lawyer well known for his defence of blacks in political trials—as giving free expression to liberal principles.

She had not told, she did not know what had happened.

She thought of a time long ago when a school camp had gone to the sea and immediately on arrival everyone had run down to the beach from the train, tripping and tearing over sand dunes of wild fig, aghast with ecstatic shock at the meeting with the water.

De Poorteer was recalled and the lawyer remarked to one of their black friends, 'The crane has choked on the bullfrog. I hear that's what they're saying in the Quarter.'

The priest who came from the black slum that had always been known simply by that anonymous term did not respond with any sort of glee. His reserve implied it was easy to celebrate; there were people who 'shouted freedom too loud all of a sudden'.

The lawyer and his wife understood: Father Mulumbua was one who had shouted freedom when it was dangerous to do so, and gone to prison several times for it, while certain people, now on the Interim Council set up to run the country until the new government took over, had kept silent. He named a few, but reluctantly. Enough to confirm their own suspicions—men who perhaps had made some deal with the colonial power to place its interests first, no matter what sort of government might emerge from the new constitution? Yet when the couple plunged into discussion their friend left them talking to each other while he drank his beer and gazed, frowning as if at a headache or because the sunset light hurt his eyes behind his spectacles, round her huge-leaved tropical plants that bowered the terrace in cool humidity.

They had always been rather proud of their friendship with him, this man in a cassock who wore a clenched fist carved of local ebony as well as a silver cross round his neck. His black face was habitually stern—a high seriousness balanced by sudden splurting laughter when they used to tease him over the fist—but never inattentively ill-at-ease.

'What was the matter?' She answered herself; 'I had the feeling he didn't want to come here.' She was using a paper handkerchief dipped in gin to wipe greenfly off the back of a pale new leaf that had shaken itself from its folds like a cut-out paper lantern.

'Good lord, he's been here hundreds of times.'

'—Before, yes.'

What things were they saying?

With the shouting in the street and the swaying of the crowd, the sweet powerful presence that confused the senses so that sound, sight, stink (sweat, cheap soap) ran into one tremendous sensation, she could not make out words that came so easily.

Not even what she herself must have said.

A few wealthy white men who had been boastful in their support of the colonial war and knew they would be marked down by the blacks as arch exploiters, left at once. Good riddance, as the lawyer and his wife remarked. Many ordinary white people who had lived contentedly, without questioning its actions, under the colonial government, now expressed an enthusiastic intention to help build a nation, as the newspapers put it. The lawyer's wife's neighbourhood butcher was one. 'I don't mind blacks.' He was expansive with her, in his shop that he had occupied for twelve years on a licence available only to white people. 'Makes no difference to me who you are so long as you're honest.' Next to a chart showing a beast mapped according to the cuts of meat it provided, he had hung a picture of the most important leader of the freedom fighters, expected to be first President. People like the butcher turned out with their babies clutching pennants when the leader drove through the town from the airport.

There were incidents (newspaper euphemism again) in the Quarter. It was to be expected. Political factions, tribally based, who had not fought the war, wanted to share power with the freedom fighters' Party. Muchanga no longer went down to the Quarter on his day off. His friends came to see him and sat privately on their hunkers near the garden compost heap. The ugly mansions of the rich who had fled stood empty on the bluff above the sea, but it was said they would make money out of them yet —they would be bought as ambassadorial residences when independence came, and with it many black and yellow diplomats. Zealots who claimed they belonged to the Party burned shops and houses of the poorer whites who lived, as the lawyer said, 'in the inevitable echelon of colonial society', closest to the Quarter. A house in the lawyer's street was noticed by his wife to be accommodating what was certainly one of those families, in the outhouses; green nylon curtains had appeared at the garage window, she reported. The suburb was pleasantly overgrown and well-to-do; no one rich, just white professional people and professors from the university. The barracks was empty now, except for an old man with a stump and a police uniform stripped of insignia, a friend of Muchanga, it turned out, who sat on a beer-crate at the gates. He had lost his job as night-watchman when one of the rich people went away, and was glad to have work.

The street had been perfectly quiet; except for that first day.

The fingernails she sometimes still saw clearly were bitten down until embedded in a thin line of dirt all round, in the pink blunt fingers. The thumb and thick fingertips were turned back coarsely even while grasping her. Such hands had never been allowed to take possession. They were permanently raw, so young, from unloading coal, digging potatoes from the frozen Northern Hemisphere, washing hotel dishes. He had not been killed, and now that day of the cease-fire was over he would be delivered back across the sea to the docks, the stony farm, the scullery of the grand hotel. He would have to do anything he could get. There was unemployment in Europe where he had returned, the army didn't need all the young men any more.

A great friend of the lawyer and his wife, Chipande, was coming home from exile. They heard over the radio he was expected, accompanying the future President as confidential secretary, and they waited to hear from him.

The lawyer put up his feet on the empty chair where the priest had sat, shifting it to a comfortable position by hooking his toes, free in sandals, through the slats. 'Imagine, Chipande!' Chipande had been almost a protégé—but they didn't like the term, it smacked of patronage. Tall, cocky, casual Chipande, a boy from the slummiest part of the Quarter, was recommended by the White Fathers' Mission (was it by Father Mulumbua himself?— the lawyer thought so, his wife was not sure they remembered correctly) as a bright kid who wanted to be articled to a lawyer. That was asking a lot, in those days—nine years ago. He never finished his apprenticeship because while he and his employer were soon close friends, and the kid picked up political theories from the books in the house he made free of, he became so involved in politics that he had to skip the country one jump ahead of a detention order signed by the crane-who-was-trying-to-swallow-the-bullfrog.

After two weeks, the lawyer phoned the offices the guerilla-movement-become-Party had set up openly in the town but apparently Chipande had an office in the former colonial secretariat. There he had a secretary of his own; he wasn't easy to reach. The lawyer left a message. The lawyer and his wife saw from the newspaper pictures he hadn't changed much: he had a beard and had adopted the Muslim cap favoured by political circles in exile on the East Coast.

He did come to the house eventually. He had the distracted, insistent friendliness of one who has no time to re-establish intimacy; it must be taken as read. And it must not be displayed. When he remarked on a shortage of accommodation for exiles now become officials, and the lawyer said the house was far too big for two people, he was welcome to move in and regard a self-contained part of it as his private living quarters, he did not answer but went on talking generalities. The lawyer's wife mentioned Father Mulumbua, whom they had not seen since just after the cease-fire. The lawyer added, 'There's obviously some sort of big struggle going on, he's fighting for his political life there in the Quarter.' 'Again,' she said, drawing them into a reminder of what had only just become their past.

But Chipande was restlessly following with his gaze the movements of old Muchanga, dragging the hose from plant to plant, careless of the spray; 'You remember who this is, Muchanga?' she had said when the visitor arrived, yet although the old man had given, in their own language, the sort of respectful greeting even an elder gives a young man whose clothes and bearing denote rank and authority, he was not in any way overwhelmed nor enthusiastic—perhaps he secretly supported one of the rival factions?

The lawyer spoke of the latest whites to leave the country—people who had got themselves quickly involved in the sort of currency swindle that draws more outrage than any other kind of crime, in a new state fearing the flight of capital: 'Let them go, let them go. Good riddance.' And he turned to talk of other things—there were so many more important questions to occupy the attention of the three old friends.

But Chipande couldn't stay. Chipande could not stay for supper; his beautiful long velvety black hands with their pale lining (as she thought of the palms) hung impatiently between his knees while he sat forward in the chair, explaining, adamant against persuasion. He should not have been there, even now; he had official business waiting, sometimes he drafted correspondence until one or two in the morning. The lawyer remarked how there hadn't been a proper chance to talk; he wanted to discuss those fellows in the Interim Council Mulumbua was so warily distrustful of—what did Chipande know?

Chipande, already on his feet, said something dismissing and very slightly disparaging, not about the Council members but of Mulumbua—a reference to his connection with the Jesuit missionaries as an influence that 'comes through'. 'But I must make a note to see him sometime.'

It seemed that even black men who presented a threat to the Party could be discussed only among black men themselves, now. Chipande put an arm round each of his friends as for the brief official moment of a photograph, left them; he who used to sprawl on the couch arguing half the night before dossing down in the lawyer's pyjamas. 'As soon as I'm settled I'll contact you. You'll be around, ay?'

'Oh we'll be around.' The lawyer laughed, referring, for his part, to those who were no longer. 'Glad to see you're not driving a Mercedes!' he called with reassured affection at the sight of Chipande getting into a modest car. How many times, in the old days, had they agreed on the necessity for African leaders to live simply when they came to power!

On the terrace to which he turned back, Muchanga was doing something extraordinary—wetting a dirty rag with Gilbey's. It was supposed to be his day off, anyway; why was he messing about with the plants when one wanted peace to talk undisturbed?

'Is those thing again, those thing is killing the leaves.'

'For heaven's sake, he could use methylated for that! Any kind of alcohol will do! Why don't you get him some?'

There were shortages of one kind and another in the country, and gin happened to be something in short supply.

Whatever the hand had done in the bush had not coarsened it. It, too, was suède-black, and elegant. The pale lining was hidden against her own skin where the hand grasped her left elbow. Strangely, black does not show toil—she remarked this as one remarks the quality of a fabric. The hand was not as long but as distinguished by beauty as Chipande's. The watch a fine piece of equipment for a fighter. There was something next to it, in fact looped over the strap by the angle of the wrist as the hand grasped. A bit of thong with a few beads knotted where it was joined as a bracelet. Or amulet. Their babies wore such things; often their first and only garment. Grandmothers or mothers attached it as protection. It had worked; he was alive at cease-fire. Some had been too deep in the bush to know, and had been killed after the fighting was over. He had pumped his head wildly and laughingly at whatever it was she—they—had been babbling.

The lawyer had more free time than he'd ever remembered. So many of his clients had left; he was deputed to collect their rents and pay their taxes for them, in the hope that their property wasn't going to be confiscated—there had been alarmist rumours among such people since the day of the cease-fire. But without the rich whites there was little litigation over possessions, whether in the form of the children of dissolved marriages or the houses and cars claimed by divorced wives. The Africans had their own ways of resolving such redistribution of goods. And a gathering of elders under a tree was sufficient to settle a dispute over boundaries or argue for and against the guilt of a woman accused of adultery. He had had a message, in a round-about way, that he might be asked to be consultant on constitutional law to the Party, but nothing seemed to come of it. He took home with him the proposals for the draft constitution he had managed to get hold of. He spent whole afternoons in his study making notes for counter or improved proposals he thought he would send to Chipande or one of the other people he knew in high positions: every time he glanced up, there through his open windows was Muchanga's little company at the bottom of the garden. Once, when he saw they had straggled off, he wandered down himself to clear his head (he got drowsy, as he never did when he used to work twelve hours a day at the office). They ate dried shrimps, from the market: that's what they were doing! The ground was full of bitten-off heads and black eyes on stalks. His wife smiled. 'They bring them. Muchanga won't go near the market since the riot.' 'It's ridiculous. Who's going to harm him?'

17

There was even a suggestion that the lawyer might apply for a professorship at the university. The chair of the Faculty of Law was vacant, since the students had demanded the expulsion of certain professors engaged during the colonial regime—in particular of the fuddy-duddy (good riddance) who had gathered dust in the Law chair, and the quite decent young man (pity about him) who had had Political Science. But what professor of Political Science could expect to survive both a colonial regime and the revolutionary regime that defeated it? The lawyer and his wife decided that since he might still be appointed in some consultative capacity to the new government it would be better to keep out of the university context, where the students were shouting for Africanization, and even an appointee with his credentials as a fighter of legal battles for blacks against the colonial regime in the past might not escape their ire.

Newspapers sent by friends from over the border gave statistics for the number of what they termed 'refugees' who were entering the neighbouring country. The papers from outside also featured sensationally the inevitable mistakes and misunderstandings, in a new administration, that led to several foreign businessmen being held for investigation by the new regime. For the last fifteen years of colonial rule, Gulf had been drilling for oil in the territory, and just as inevitably it was certain that all sorts of questionable people, from the point of view of the regime's determination not to be exploited preferentially, below the open market for the highest bidder in ideological as well as economic terms, would try to gain concessions.

His wife said, 'The butcher's gone.'

He was home, reading at his desk; he could spend the day more usefully there than at the office, most of the time. She had left after breakfast with her fisherman's basket that she liked to use for shopping, she wasn't away twenty minutes. 'You mean the shop's closed?' There was nothing in the basket. She must have turned and come straight home.

'Gone. It's empty. He's cleared out over the weekend.'

She sat down suddenly on the edge of the desk; and after a moment of silence, both laughed shortly, a strange, secret, complicit laugh. 'Why, do you think?' 'Can't say. He certainly charged, if you wanted a decent cut. But meat's so hard to get, now; I thought it was worth it—justified.'

The lawyer raised his eyebrows and pulled down his mouth: 'Exactly.' They understood; the man probably knew he was marked to run into trouble for profiteering—he must have been paying through the nose for his supplies on the black market, anyway, didn't have much choice.

Shops were being looted by the unemployed and loafers (there had always been a lot of unemployed hanging around for the pickings of the town) who felt the new regime should entitle them to take what they dared not before. Radio and television shops were the most favoured objective for gangs who adopted the freedom fighters' slogans. Transistor radios were the portable luxuries of street life; the new regime issued solemn warnings, over those same radios, that looting and violence would be firmly dealt with but it was difficult for the police to be everywhere at once. Sometimes their actions became street battles, since the struggle with the looters changed character as supporters of the Party's rival political factions joined in with the thieves against the police. It was necessary to be ready to reverse direction, quickly turning down a side street in detour if one encountered such disturbances while driving around town. There were bodies sometimes; both husband and wife had been fortunate enough not to see any close up, so far. A company of the freedom fighters' army was brought down from the north and installed in the barracks to supplement the police force; they patrolled the Quarter, mainly. Muchanga's friend kept his job as gatekeeper although there were armed sentries on guard: the lawyer's wife found that a light touch to mention in letters to relatives in Europe.

'Where'll you go now?'

She slid off the desk and picked up her basket. 'Supermarket, I suppose. Or turn vegetarian.' He knew that she left the room quickly, smiling, because she didn't want him to suggest Muchanga ought to be sent to look for fish in the markets along the wharf in the Quarter. Muchanga was being allowed to indulge in all manner of eccentric refusals; for no reason, unless out of some curious sentiment about her father?

She avoided walking past the barracks because of the machine guns the young sentries had in place of rifles. Rifles pointed into the air but machine guns pointed to the street at the level of different parts of people's bodies, short and tall, the backsides of babies slung on mothers' backs, the round heads of children, her fisherman's basket—she knew she was getting like the others: what she felt was afraid. She wondered what the butcher and his wife had said to each other. Because he was at least one whom she had known. He had sold the meat she had bought that these women and their babies passing her in the street didn't have the money to buy.

It was something quite unexpected and outside their own efforts that decided it. A friend over the border telephoned and offered a place in a lawyers' firm of highest repute there, and some prestige in the world at large, since the team had defended individuals fighting for freedom of the press and militant churchmen upholding freedom of conscience on political issues. A telephone call; as simple as that. The friend said (and the lawyer did not repeat this even to his wife) they would be proud to have a man of his courage and convictions in the firm. He could be satisfied he would be able to uphold the liberal principles everyone knew he had always stood for; there were many whites, in that country still ruled by a white minority, who deplored the injustices under which their black population suffered etc. and believed you couldn't ignore the need for peaceful change etc.

His offices presented no problem; something called Africa Seabeds (Formosan Chinese who had gained a concession to ship seaweed and dried shrimps in exchange for rice) took over the lease and the typists. The senior clerks and the current articled clerk (the lawyer had always given a chance to young blacks, long before other people had come round to it—it wasn't only the secretary to the President who owed his start to him) he managed to get employed by the new Trades Union Council; he still knew a few blacks who remembered the times he had acted for black workers in disputes with the colonial government. The house would just have to stand empty, for the time being. It wasn't imposing enough to attract an embassy but maybe it would do for a Chargé d'Affaires —it was left in the hands of a half-caste letting agent who was likely to stay put: only whites were allowed in, at the country over the border. Getting money out was going to be much more difficult than disposing of the house. The lawyer would have to keep coming back, so long as this remained practicable, hoping to find a loophole in exchange control regulations.

She was deputed to engage the movers. In their innocence, they had thought it as easy as that! Every large vehicle, let alone a pantechnicon, was commandeered for months ahead. She had no choice but to grease a palm, although it went against her principles, it was condoning a practice they believed a young black state must stamp out before corruption took hold. He would take his entire legal library, for a start; that was the most important possession, to him. Neither was particularly attached to furniture. She did not know what there was she felt she really could not do without. Except the plants. And that was out of the question. She could not even mention it. She did not want to leave her towering plants, mostly natives of South America and not Africa, she supposed, whose aerial tubes pushed along the terrace brick erect tips extending hourly in the growth of the rainy season, whose great leaves turned shields to the spatter of Muchanga's hose glancing off in a shower of harmless arrows, whose two-hand-span trunks were smooth and grooved in one sculptural sweep down their length, or carved by the drop of each dead leaf-stem with concave medallions marking the place and building a pattern at once bold and exquisite. Such things would not travel; they were too big to give away.

The evening she was beginning to pack the books, the telephone rang in the study. Chipande—and he called her by her name, urgently, commandingly—'What is this all about? Is it true, what I hear? Let me just talk to him—'

'Our friend,' she said, making a long arm, receiver at the end of it, towards her husband.

'But you can't leave!' Chipande shouted down the phone. '*You* can't go! I'm coming round. *Now*.'

She went on packing the legal books while Chipande and her husband were shut up together in the living-room.

'He cried. You know, he actually cried.' Her husband stood in the doorway, alone.

'I know—that's what I've always liked so much about them, whatever they do. They feel.'

The lawyer made a face: there it is, it happened; hard to believe.

'Rushing in here, after nearly a year! I said, but we haven't seen you, all this time...he took no notice. Suddenly he starts pressing me to take the university job, raising all sorts of objections, why not this...that. And then he really wept, for a moment.'

They got on with packing books like builder and mate deftly handling and catching bricks.

And the morning they were to leave it was all done; twenty-one years of life in that house gone quite easily into one pantechnicon. They were quiet with each other, perhaps out of apprehension of the tedious search of their possessions that would take place at the border; it was said that if you struck over-conscientious or officious freedom fighter patrols they would even make you unload a piano, a refrigerator or washing machine. She had bought Muchanga a hawker's licence, a hand-cart, and stocks of small commodities. Now that many small shops owned by white shopkeepers had disappeared, there was an opportunity for humble itinerant black traders. Muchanga had lost his fear of the town. He was proud of what she had done for him and she knew he saw himself as a rich merchant; this was the only sort of freedom he understood, after so many years as a servant. But she also knew, and the lawyer sitting beside her in the car knew she knew, that the shortages of the goods Muchanga could sell from his cart, the sugar and soap and matches and pomade and sunglasses, would soon put him out of business. He promised to come back to the house and look after the plants every week; and he stood waving, as he had done every year when they set off on holiday. She did not know what to call out to him as they drove away. The right words would not come again; whatever they were, she left them behind.

A LION ON THE FREEWAY

O pen up!
   Open up!
What hammered on the door of sleep?
Who's that?

Anyone who lives within a mile of the zoo hears lions on summer nights. A tourist could be fooled. Africa already; at last; even though he went to bed in yet another metropole.

Just before light, when it's supposed to be darkest, the body's at its lowest ebb and in the hospital on the hill old people die—the night opens, a Black Hole between stars, and from it comes a deep panting. Very distant and at once very close, right in the ear, for the sound of breath is always intimate. It grows and grows, deeper, faster, more rasping, until a great groan, a rising groan lifts out of the curved bars of the cage and hangs above the whole city—

And then drops back, sinks away, becomes panting again.

Wait for it; it will fall so quiet, hardly more than a faint roughness snagging the air in the ear's chambers. Just when it seems to have sunk between strophe and antistrophe, a breath is taken and it gasps once; pauses, sustaining the night as a singer holds a note. And begins once more. The panting reaches up up up down down down to that awe-ful groan—

Open up!
Open up!
Open your legs.

In the geriatric wards where lights are burning they take the tubes out of noses and the saline-drip needles out of arms and draw the sheets to cover faces. I pull the sheet over my head. I can smell

my own breath caught there. It's very late; it's much too early to
be awake. Sometimes the rubber tyres of the milk truck rolled over
our sleep. You turned...

Roar is not the word. Children learn not to hear for themselves,
doing exercises in the selection of verbs at primary school: 'Complete these sentences: The cat ...s The dog ...s The lion ...s.'
Whoever decided that had never listened to the real thing. The
verb is onomatopoeically incorrect just as the heraldic beasts drawn
by thirteenth- and fourteenth-century engravers at second hand
from the observations of early explorers are anatomically wrong.
Roar is not the word for the sound of great chaps sucking in and
out the small hours.

The zoo lions do not utter during the day. They yawn; wait
for their ready-slaughtered kill to be tossed at them; keep their
unused claws sheathed in huge harmless pads on which top-
heavy, untidy heads rest (the visualized lion is always a maned
male), gazing through lid-slats with what zoo visitors think of in
sentimental prurience as yearning.

Or once we were near the Baltic and the leviathan hooted from
the night fog at sea. But would I dare to open my mouth now?
Could I trust my breath to be sweet, these stale nights?

It's only on warm summer nights that the lions are restless.
What they're seeing when they gaze during the day is nothing,
their eyes are open but they don't see us—you can tell that when
the lens of the pupil suddenly shutters at the close swoop of one
of the popcorn-begging pigeons through the bars of the cage.
Otherwise the eye remains blank, registering nothing. The lions
were born in the zoo (for a few brief weeks the cubs are on show
to the public, children may hold them in their arms). They know
nothing but the zoo; they are not expressing our yearnings. It's
only on certain nights that their muscles flex and they begin to

pant, their flanks heave as if they had been running through the dark night while other creatures shrank from their path, their jaws hang tense and wet as saliva flows as if in response to a scent of prey, at last they heave up their too-big heads, heavy, heavy heads, and out it comes. Out over the suburbs. A dreadful straining of the bowels to deliver itself: a groan that hangs above the houses in a low-lying cloud of smog and anguish.

O Jack, O Jack, O Jack, oh—I heard it once through a hotel wall. Was alone and listened. Covers drawn over my head and knees drawn up to my fists. Eyes strained wide open. Sleep again!—my command. *Sleep again.*

It must be because of the new freeway that they are not heard so often lately. It passes its five-lane lasso close by, drawing in the valley between the zoo and the houses on the ridge. There is traffic there very late, too early. Trucks. Tankers, getting a start before daylight. The rising spray of rubber spinning friction on tarmac is part of the quality of city silence; after a time you don't hear much beyond it. But sometimes—perhaps it's because of a breeze. Even on a still summer night there must be some sort of breeze opening up towards morning. Not enough to stir the curtains, a current of air has brought, small, clear and distant, right into the ear, the sound of panting.

Or perhaps the neat whisky after dinner. The rule is don't drink after dinner. A metabolic switch trips in the brain: open up.

Who's that?

A truck of potatoes going through traffic lights quaked us sixteen flights up.

Slack with sleep, I was impaled in the early hours. You grew like a tree and lifted the pavements; everything rose, cracked, and split free.

Who's that?

Or something read in the paper... Yes. Last night—this night—in the City Late, front page, there were the black strikers in the streets, dockers with sticks and knobkerries. A thick prancing black centipede with thousands of waving legs advancing. The panting grows louder, it could be in the garden or under the window; there comes that pause, that slump of breath. Wait for it: waiting for it. Prance, advance, over the carefully-tended please keep off the grass. They went all through a city not far from this one, their steps are so rhythmical, waving sticks (no spears any more, no guns yet); they can cover any distance, in time. Shops and houses closed against them while they passed. And the cry that came from them as they approached—that groan straining, the rut of freedom bending the bars of the cage, he's delivered himself of it, it's as close as if he's out on the freeway now, bewildered, finding his way, turning his splendid head at last to claim what he's never seen, the country where he's king.

SIBLINGS

Fifteen was three years short of the minimum age for a driver's licence but he drove the Mini through the quieter streets of the Johannesburg suburb when he was home in the school holidays and several times he saw her—unmistakably her. Hobbling along in a trailing skirt. Those shoes made her feet look like a dray-horse's hooves; above them, the layers of clothing both skimpy and voluminous, blouse shining with tiny Indian mirrors, washer-woman's crocheted shawl, clung and drooped around her body. She had got thin again. Sometimes (usually when she had come out of a clinic, he understood) she was, horribly, almost fat and jolly, with those fresh scars nobody looked at on the inner side of her wrists. She walked as tramps do, and children let out of school: people who are not going anywhere. Simply alive in the street, into which she seemed to have wandered between one night and the next—her mime's makeup and neon-tinted hair would compose a readable face under indoor lighting.

He didn't have to stop and speak to her if he didn't want to. She never saw him; she didn't notice anything or anyone, existing in flirtatious defiance purely as an object other people must be looking at (you could see in the set of her head she was sure of it). A wonder she didn't get run over.

Nothing will happen to her, his mother said, in one of those set pieces of family discussion that are the dark side of family jokes— just as repetitious, inevitable, and without hope of a fresh denoue-ment. She will kill my sister, that's all, his mother said. His father became silent once practical measures were not being discussed; such emotionalism was a woman's thing, along with menstruation and giving birth. He himself was silent because when his mother spoke like this, so venomously, with an unconscious tremor of the head (one of those mascots with neck affixed to a hidden spring within the body that bob in the rear window of some people's cars), she was not his mother but a woman, a being finally separated from himself.

There was another set piece:
You realize if he runs into somebody the insurance won't pay.
He really is very careful.
It's not a matter of what he does. If someone bumps him, he's the one who's committing the offence, no right to be on the road at all. You're encouraging him to break the law.
All right. It's not so serious. If that's the only law he breaks, we...
He isn't taking drugs and hanging around with the motorbike crowd. Consider yourself lucky. Only just here in our own suburb...

What was *she* doing, in the suburbs she had so determinedly outcast herself from, anyway? What did she want back here, outside the white walls with hanging gardens of bougainvillaea, and the plaster doves and classical urns above handsome teak gates bearing plates: BEWARE OF THE DOG THIS PROPERTY PROTECTED BY VIGILANTE RADIO BURGLAR ALARMS. The mystery of her existence reminded him of her: they had, by consensus—the whole family—at last reluctantly given up, let her go, cut her out of their lives because they couldn't help her; yet there she was. Every morning when he got up in the clamour of bells and voices at school, or here at home deliciously slowly, looking at the clock-hand made by a rod of light through the curtain-gap pointing to the angle of at least ten or half-past, she was beginning a day—somewhere. What sort of day? The terrible things they all knew had happened to her, the afternoon when the woman who did her washing found her snoring unconscious beside an empty bottle of sleeping pills, the day when she had just strength enough to phone a friend and whisper she had cut her wrists again, the times she had sent desperate appeals (turning from members of the family to distant collaterals as each in succession had 'had enough of her') from police stations where she was under arrest on drug charges, or from the closed sections of psychiatric clinics he imagined to be worse than jails; such days, swollen and siren in his mind with the panic wah-awah-awah-awah of police cars and ambulances—such days could bear no relation to everyday. Not in his life, or the life of anyone he knew. But hers was one, he was told the doctors said, where every day might be at this breath-holding, lung-bursting pitch. Reminded of her; yes, she had terrified him, when she was seven and he about four, by holding her breath with her mouth opened in a soundless scream when they quarrelled at play. Her face, going steadily purple-black round that mouth, was always directed straight at him. When tears bulged at last out of her eyes he felt something had burst in her but at least she was alive.

Alive still; although that childhood they had lived together as more than cousins—her mother and his were identical twins, so that the children were attached, so to speak, one to either breast of the same sustaining being—had opened out around him securely, while she had slit it as a mercenary's bayonet does a womb, and torn herself out, bloody. He asked where Maxine was living now? Well, nobody had heard from her for months, so that meant at least she hadn't been in trouble, she only bothered to make contact when there was a crisis; the last anyone knew was that she had moved into some Hillbrow flat with a woman. That was the latest; she tormented her mother, at a distance, by boasting that she was living as a Lesbian, now. And what did the psychiatrist say? The psychiatrist! (His mother treated him as an adult, she didn't believe in trying to conceal anything from him.) The psychiatrist! That child twists him round her little finger! You know how she's always been. Turns on the charm and lies and cheats and wheedles, and he becomes her victim, like everybody else. She won't rest until she's destroyed him, too—his professional detachment. Just as she kills everything she needs. As she's destroyed my poor sister.

He said, What happened about R. D. Laing?

From time to time, between dropping the question of her existence altogether, there were these discussions to decide what ought to be done with his cousin. Last holidays there was a suggestion that she might be sent to England to be treated. This woman sitting on the terrace with him, whom, as a child, he had shared indiscriminately as mother with the little girl, was the one who had been supposed to be looking into the possibility. But it seemed the Laing Institute was no longer run by the famous man himself. The mother was talking about a letter of advice from someone else with first-hand experience of 'disturbed' people: ...Lemaître said it would have to be someone—but not her own mother, too late for that, that's out—someone who would stand in relation to her as mother, a family that would provide her with a family, and then one must be prepared to take *everything*. Accept. No matter what. One word: accept. Anything she does. It might take years, might not even be successful then, yet it's the only way. —But what about the other people? If she were to smash—that whole family? In the process? What about them?— And Lemaître said, yes, that is what I mean: you take her on and you let her do her worst. It's the only way you can help her. You take her on, and if you can't stand it, you have to tell her: go.

The two were alone in the sun, smoking; he did not do so in front of his father, who objected for health reasons. The dog came and nudged its nose into his rich-smelling adolescent armpit; but his mother would not allow the question of this existence to lapse (once again, as it must) without his complicity. If he had shared his mother, he had done so with someone who was, by the same process, a sister.

It's out of the question. Mmmh? You might do it for a man... Or a woman—you might take it on if the person were to be some-one you were in love with. Just might. But who could be expected—

He pulled the dog away, then tenderly wiped its wet eyes with its long ears. She waited for his answer and he looked at her, the look she was waiting for. She said, It's unnatural. Only saints. —In a moment she put out her cigarette and followed by the dog went away into the house carrying the stub, because she disliked people leaving cigarette ends in the terrace pot-plants.

They didn't know so it didn't harm them, but of course he did drive to crowded Hillbrow and to town sometimes. What was there to see in the suburbs, with everyone hidden away in private gardens? And in Hillbrow at eleven o'clock one morning he had the amused pleasure of tooting her out of her skin as she stepped off a kerb just where he was manoeuvring into a parking space. It was like the times when he would drop from a tree in front of her, when they were little kids. She turned a proud, furious, disdainful face; and then—his blast the trump at which the whole cast of the present fell from her—there emerged not just a smile, her big smile, but a face of pure joy.

You little devil! My Lord Muck! Look who's driving around in cars!

She had a fat friend with her, a girl who hung back patiently on the kerb. Most of her friends were like that, following round in the trance of her domination. She said, and then scarcely bothered to address the girl again, This's my cousin, Patrick, we used to play 'doctor' together for hours—her eyes opened, enormous, her pale orange Dietrich brows went up like a clown's, her mouth became a huge parody-reproachful, upside-down U—Patty, remember? Naughty naughty, let's touch wees? Oh-hh-hh—And the pallor was gone, she mimed, she laughed, her face was gay and rosy with the buffeting of laughter, her hands were on her half-starved hips, bracelets slopping over the wrists, she rocked from the waist and of course everybody turned to look at that wild girl, there in the street; but perhaps she really was not needing them to clothe her with their curious gaze, this time.

Come, Patty-cake, you're so rich and so GROWN-UP, you are going to buy us doughnuts and coffee—and she took his arm and bent her head as she swept him along, looking up into his face from under long coppery hair. It took her fancy to assert and caricature the simple fact of her three years' seniority (today was not a time when that other seniority, of disgrace and suffering, was taken into account); the only other woman he'd ever escorted like that was an aunt with a gammy leg.

I have a passion for doughnuts. Yesterday I ate—how many was it, four in the morning and five in the afternoon?—yes, I promise you—how many doughnuts did I eat yesterday? But while the fat friend was trying to guess at the reply expected of her, it was not waited for. No, you must order at least three for me—I'm perfectly serious—and one will do for her, she's on a diet. From today. I'm putting her on a *strict* diet. But they're de-licious here, you'll see. There's a gorgeous gob of real apricot jam in the centre.

She was responding to greetings, some flamboyant, some merely laconic signals, all over the coffee bar. He saw for himself evidence of the existence of the days she woke up to, in the quick—and as quickly vanished—changes in her face as she pursed her mouth in popping kisses, lifted a limp hand, raised both palms declamatorily over her head, or showed (the point of a knife) a downglance that pretended not to notice at all.

I like your hair, Max. You've let it grow.

She smiled at him sweetly. You do, Patrick? You really think it suits me?

Well, that time—at Christmas? It was frizzed. And an awful colour.

Oh I know. I was a sight. I had to turn up and spoil the Christmas table, the crackers and streamers, the flowers and the Cries of London place-mats with my ghastly ghoulish hair. Oh I *know*.

Only he would recognize the confidential false-teeth sibilance as that of an old friend of the family who would raise her voice cheerfully, as you entered the room, to disguise what had been said behind the young people's backs. While Maxine was mimicking gossip about herself her hands were going about the things on the table, helping herself greedily to unappetizing balls smelling of fat and sugar; he always tried not to look in the region of those hands, because of the wrists and also because they shook like an old person's, cigarettes and cups trembled in a perpetually shivering grasp, so that even while she made you laugh, her hands suggested that she was terrified. Now these wavering hands went from the doughnuts up to her head, in the customary vain gesture of long-haired young girls, and in an instant had whipped off the hair, doffed it like a splendid, plumed hat, and revealed an almost naked skull covered with tufts curled and dyed sunset-yellow.

The friend concertinaed upon her own bulges in outraged laughter. There was applause somewhere above the yelling from the juke box. Someone shouted, Oh Christ, not Maxine— A grandmother in a smart trouser-suit who was treating children to ice-cream was pestered by their scandalized and delighted curiosity: What's the matter with the lady? But what's the lady doing? Then the littlest one started to cry, tugging at her own hair: Sore! Sore!

The wig was laid upon the fourth chair at the table and smoothed, a pet dog. The blazing sunset head on a frail neck concentrated perfectly on the task of stuffing away doughnuts. He knew that when she was taking pills she didn't eat for days but when you saw how she still could eat, you felt there was nothing much wrong with her, after all.

It didn't really work, Max, because I've seen you a few times. Lately. Hair couldn't have grown that quickly. Even I'm not such a dope...though for a moment I did forget...I saw you the other week near our place.

Oh if I'd've known you were back from school! I'd have come in. Really. How's everyone? You must come to my flat, ay, Patty—you must. It's just near the fire station—you know? Penarth Mansions. An old, old building. Don't go through the front entrance, it's quicker up the fire escape on the right. First door facing you on the first floor. There's someone else's name on the door but don't worry. The caretaker's an old cow who didn't want to let me have the place, so we got a friend to take it and then just moved in. Come anytime, ay? —Give them my love.

Well thank God for doughnuts. A harmless enough addiction. She say anything about this woman she's living with?

A fat girl was with her; but that couldn't be the one.

Ironic levity suddenly failed. His mother said with distasteful anguish, It's terrible, in its way, that gorging. Infantile. A sign of such deprivation, regression. She craves—I don't know. Neither my sister nor the doctors or anyone else— Is there any difference, for her, between swallowing Mandrax or sugar doughnuts?

He himself felt a weariness, a childish jealousy: so far as he was concerned, he had seen Maxine eating doughnuts with the relish of one of the junior boys at school, jam oozing between her teeth and sugar bristling on her lips. And his mother was so intelligent, she could analyse and explain everything but that was the end of it; she couldn't tell anyone what to do.

Max sends her love, anyway.

Oh love! I'm tired of hearing about love! A bill that doesn't say what it was contracted for and where or how or in what currency it's got to be paid. Run to more doctors and ask them. Isn't that what her parents have been doing for four years. Love. Makes me shudder. She gets herself beaten up in a Hillbrow dive. You should have seen her poor jaw. Her father has to get up at two o'clock in the morning to bail her out of a police station. She blackmails *your* father—yes, that's what it is, though poor little devil, she doesn't realize the ugly name for it—when she's prosecuted for wrecking a flat and she knows we'll do anything to protect my sister. Her love. Oh poor little creature.

But they were pleased he had made contact—as they put it—with Maxine. He could imagine the conversations because he knew how they would go: who knows, perhaps someone near her own age…? He may be able to reach her in a way we can't. They felt they had at least appointed an emissary to territory where they themselves would not venture.

They didn't ask, and he did not tell them whether or not he made efforts to see his cousin again. A quiet period continued. Delicately (not to disturb the calm under which that *existence* lay —treasure or drowned Ophelia with the mime's public face), his mother rubbed the ridge of her nose with her forefinger: What shall we do about Maxine's birthday?

He never remembered any birthday but his own. Her birthday? When?

But don't you know? The sixteenth. Thursday.

Oh yes. She'll be nineteen.

And he was thinking, that means I'll soon be sixteen; only two more years and I'll have a licence.

Maxine's own parents would have to ignore the birthday; they were trying another interpretation of love—the strength to cut oneself off entirely.

Nothing was decided. The small problem slid away under others. But on Thursday morning his mother came in when he was having late breakfast. You know where Maxine lives, don't you? I must take the kid something. It's too dismal to have one's birthday ignored.

Penarth Mansions. The old building near the fire station.

You come with me, she said. Come and give her a birthday kiss. She used to love her birthday parties, showing off, such a pretty little girl and you used to say to me—

It's all a hundred years ago.

Oh I don't mean anything sentimental—I just want to acknowledge she has a birthday like anyone else, and people take the trouble to remember it.

Okay, okay, don't eat me up.

The next problem was what to buy as a present.

Something for the flat? But she's constantly moving, isn't she, that would be out of place, she'd laugh behind our backs.

Why should she *laugh*. You don't understand; she isn't scornful about people like you and Dad and her parents, she's not spiteful. It's herself she's always jeering at. But it's just that she doesn't need things like—towels and things—it's one room—

He did not say that he had been to the flat only once, and Maxine was out; he had sat an hour, waiting, with the chap who was sharing the flat, her boy-friend, he supposed. They looked much the same, he and the boy-friend; both long-haired and wearing shabby boots whose toes had turned up comically with long wear, but the boy-friend had a silky black moustache and he'd taken the fancy to draw a black line round his eyes; a man of twenty or so. They talked about stock-car racing; he had been or was a special tune-up mechanic and had even owned a racing car. Maxine did not appear. That's how she is, the mouth under the black moustache pronounced, somehow independent of the unchanging inexpressiveness of the rest of the face—You never know with her. Sometimes I don't see her for days. But she'll come right. She just needs someone, like, who won't stand any crap from her. They drank two beers apiece and listened to David Cassidy records; —She plays them half the night—the whiskery moustache outlined a smile like a pleasant rat's.

In a shop his mother felt would have the sort of thing his cousin would like, they looked at all the out-of-date popular talismans of love, peace, and contemplation that she already had been observed to wear throughout the tumult and violence of her past four years. At last his mother decided upon a dress, a long cotton skirt and top of Indian print, and, since one never knew from one week to the next whether Maxine would be full of doughnuts or emaciated as a *Vogue* model—if, alas, not for reasons of fashion—arranged that she could exchange it if it didn't fit. Then they drove to the flat and their footfalls rang in silence up the fire escape to the door. At ten in the morning there were sounds of a party going on on the other side but when the door was opened by a young black woman in white plastic knee-boots and gipsy ear-rings, it was clear she was alone there, with the radio turned high to the African-language commercial programme. Like many servants, her manner towards white people was based on the personality of the white person she worked for. Her smile was Maxine's sweeping, superior yet knockabout one. Like Maxine on first-name terms with the world in which she could find no place for herself, she spoke of her employer simply as 'Maxine'. Oh Maxine'll be so sorry, so sorry. She just went out. She says to me, Dora, hang on here till I come back, won't you, because she haven't paid me this week, and she's gone out to a friend to get my money, I think. Oh she'll be so sorry.

His mother's eyes went round the one room, analysing: the bed a block of foam rubber made up on the floor, curtains on string, peacock feathers in a vase, broken suitcases, smashed mirror, but of all things a live bird in a white Tunisian cage—an old-fashioned canary, singing against the radio.

You take care of Miss Maxine?

Oh she's a good girl. You know that? She's very kind to me, Maxine. I come to do the washing every week and when she's— you know, when she's feeling well—she says to me, Dora, come let's have a party. You should see us dancing! She puts on the records and we dance together—really!

That's right, you look after Miss Maxine nicely.

And there was a rand note put easily into the graceful black hand with its broken fingernails under Maxine's brilliant green varnish.

They took the parcel with the Indian print dress away with them; there was the question of perhaps having to change it, so it would be best to drop in again on Maxine another day. They had made the effort; they had done what they could. His mother wanted to be left at the hairdresser's; he drove around on errands of

his own for a while because he would be going back to school next
week and there were certain surrogates for home, freedom, affection it was necessary to take with one—new cassettes, a blue bulb
to fix up a sexy lamp in his cubicle and (looking round the supermarket to discover the nature of his need by recognizing objects
that would seem to be fulfilling), why not?—a couple of those
throw-away cigarette lighters made in beautiful colours, purple
and lime.

He was driving slowly up his own street with his purchases
satisfyingly at his side when he saw Maxine hurrying, hobbling,
making for the house, ahead of him. By her walk—she knew where
she was going, she had a purpose, this time—by the way she swung
the yard gate and tramped in through the back as all the neighbourhood children used to do, he saw at once that Maxine was
coming for her birthday present. She had walked all the way from
Hillbrow in those heavy platform shoes to get her present. He
slowed the car to let her gain the house and be saved exposure of
this beggarly eagerness and excitement with which his eyes did
not want to shame her, as they instinctively never looked at her
wrists. She must have set out the moment she got home to the
flat and the black girl told her her aunt and cousin had come with
a parcel. At the gate he did not turn in but first drove once more,
very slowly, round the block. When he entered the house he found
the old cook Lola happily flustered, putting cheese on biscuits
for the tea-tray—he knew the kind of greeting Max always gave
her, trying to make thin arms meet round Lola's enormous waist,
hugging herself to that great, respectably undivided bosom,
kissing those smooth, innocently ageless fat cheeks as if she had
never learnt what Lola knew, that white children don't kiss their
old Lola.

You know who's here? And she's hungry, hungry—!

He took the tray and carried the birthday present beneath it to
the living-room where she was sitting as he knew she would be,
with the assurance of a movie queen in one of those old-time
pictures he and his friends loved. Over the back of the sofa, the
angle of a foot strapped high-arched to a scuffed, pea-green platform; the dyed sheepskin powder-puff that was the crown of a

head: a presence charged in smoke and a particularly pungent perfume.

She was really very thin. The bones of her hand folded together narrow as the slats of a fan in his as he gave her a birthday kiss she turned into an embrace, rocking and laughing. Look, he said, waving the parcel, we came to see you early in the morning but you were off celebrating.

Oh Patty, how marvellous, what's inside, what is it—and her one unsteady hand went out, raking a biscuit and cheese into her mouth—Mmmm—'shoft...feelsh all shoft, but nice 'n big—love big presents, mmm... She had shaken the parcel, lifted it to her ear to hear the tissue paper hissing inside, and now, gathering biscuit crumbs from round her lips with an energetic pale tongue-tip, she ripped open the wrapping and snatched out the dress.

Giving presents made him shy with responsibility. If you don't like it, just say so. Ma got the shop to promise you can take it back and get something else.

But I'm mad for it! She held the skirt against her plum velvet pants, which had given away from the fly zip, and been cobbled together with pink thread. It's divine! Aren't you crazy about it, Patrick?

If this was an act, she had the gift, the seduction, of drawing others into her fantasies. In lieu of her fat friend, he was waggling his head and laughing with her.

She took a pull at the cigarette she balanced on the table edge, shovelled more sugar into her tea and took a gulp with the spoon still upright in the cup. I can't stand these stuffy old pants. They're really for winter but I've been out of bread to get myself summer things. I'm going to put it on. I'm-not-going-to-wait-a-second.

And as she spoke she was sitting on the sofa arm prising off the shoes, heel to toe, sending them rolling over like dislodged stones, she was struggling with the pants' faulty zipper with the oblivious concentration of a little chimpanzee catching fleas in its crotch. Her feet, bare, flat on the carpet, became stubby. Pressing her thighs together to get the pants down over her body without splitting the repair, she shed them by hopping on one foot, then the other. She was naked underneath. He saw when the pale brown pubic hair appeared in the V of the open fly being pulled down past it. Lifting her arms and crossing each hand to the opposite shoulder so that her forearms momentarily hid her face, she pulled off her T-shirt as roughly, dragging up with it two brown, darker-centred circles that sprang helplessly back into place again. She was naked. The curtains at the big window were open and anyone could walk past. Even from the garden— It was the day the gardener came (Thursdays) and he could easily walk past in the woollen cap he wore winter and summer, his pipe doffed in greeting.

The boy thought immediately of that window. And the living-room door. Anyone could walk in: Lola, poor old Lola, to fetch the tea-tray. Naked; and for the moment all this presented itself as, to him, was the stark, clear window and the half-ajar door. He wanted to get up and pull the curtains but her presence itself stopped him: how she would burst out laughing, in the innocence of her nakedness, how she used to take him into the cupboard where the camping equipment was kept, holding his hand, whispering loudly straight into his face, Let's play touch wees. Hay? Shall we? —Scared?

Naked, she stood unfastening the small buttons and loops at the back of the smock-blouse with care and concentration that, along with the occasion of putting on the dress for the first time, would never be repeated. Her legs were very lightly freckled on the calves and hairless; legs looked quite different when seen in relation to the body without clothes—even the smallest bikini broke the flesh's coherence.

He had never seen a naked woman before.

He had done it with a girl—once—twice if you counted that time in the back of the combi with the other chaps, but both times were in the dark. And photographs were not the same, not the same at all. He could see that. Long ago the children must have seen their mother, but although he might have been able to remember the feel and the smell, there was nothing visual; the mother must have read in some book exactly how young a boy-child should be removed from visual Oedipal stimulation.

He was looking at the body intently as she was intently occupied with the buttons. Although he was looking at her body he was as removed from any communication with her, Maxine, as she from him, Patrick. The thighs were what would be expected, round and yet set out at that female open-angle from the soft hair that they had pressed (while a woman sits down, he supposed, legs crossed) into a sort of quiff over where the real cleft must be. But above this base a woman has, like a paperweight you can't topple, combining, even in a thin girl, the two bottom-scallops and volume of thighs, there was not what he thought there would be. The skin between hip-bones and up to the belly-button was colourless and drab, marked by wavering, shiny breaks in the tissue that looked almost blistered.

There was a blue bruise on one hip, and the sallow gooseflesh of the backside bore a long memory, at different distances of weeks? days? of other affronts, some yellow, nearly forgotten by the healed tissue, others dark, contusedly preoccupying the membranes with broken blood-vessels. The busily jerking shoulder-blades were faintly pitted here and there, the tattoo of acne or some other voracious attacker whose harm could never be made good. The diaphragm sucked in and out between ribs stretched like bony fingers under a pale kid glove; there were almost no breasts, the breasts were shrunk almost to the diameter of their big round, dark-pimpled aureoles, centred with maroon-brown nipples, pupils staring back at him—well? Well?

And she looked up now—she had finished with the buttons—and he had nothing to say. Her eyes in the painted face, the pretty, nineteen-year-old face that existed still beneath the daub she drew over it, looked at him and the two grotesque eyes of her body stared at him, all at once. He saw the puncture marks on her pale inner arms and he saw at last, slowly and lingeringly, the doctor's seams that cobbled her wrists as she had cobbled her velvet pants.

She met him calmly, without bravado but without apology, as if that other pair of blackened, battered, burnt-out eyes on her body belonged to one of those friends of hers everyone thought bad company but with whom she stood, and stood by, in disaster. She had no shame for what she had done to herself; just as because she was so afraid, so afraid, she lived as others would find it too dangerous to live.

In the movements of a few seconds the nakedness was gone. It no longer existed. The cotton skirt and smock took its place with all the mysterious authority that, he understood now, clothing had. The curly brazen head that had been decapitated by the statement of nakedness was set back on its familiar pedestal.

What he had seen for the first time was woman's nakedness, all stages of change and deterioration, of abuse and attrition by pain, loving and unloving use, he would be seeing as he lived and knew women. What he was feeling was deep distasteful awe at the knowledge of their beauty, and its decay.

When Maxine had gone he ran quickly up to his room and watched her from the window, his cousin, a girl in a cotton dress going along the road, and he thought: perhaps I'm seeing her for the last time.

TIME DID

Y ou said: '...and I'm between two girls at the moment.'
What exactly had led up to this statement that could have
come at any time, that I had been ready for so long I began to
forget it would ever come, and that you had been waiting to say
for a specific length of time I could not know? I have had great
difficulty in reconstructing exactly what had been said—begun
by me, of course, because I am always the one who speaks first
after love-making. What was said between the moment when—
feeling too warm under the covers, or looking at your sleeping or
pretending-to-be-sleeping mouth and brow—I experienced a
physical discomfort or an emotion that gave rise to speech. Say
something. How often it has happened that I surface ahead of you
from the region without words. It must have been about work—
the future of work, because that's the only future we've ever
admitted. Our future together has always been the present. I
must have said—asked—yes, that's it, whether you thought you'd
ever (now that we are middle-aged) change your job that we have
debated so long. Wanting to sleep, you answered in a way that
showed no departure from the deadlock pro-and-con we know so
well; and then there was a diversion, an exchange between us of
how successful or unsuccessful you had been in that job, anyway.
You insisted you had not reached the top of your profession. I
countered you hadn't really wanted to, had you? You had followed
that career as an avocation, your mind on the other, private work
you did at home. All the years you'd been steadily promoted: such
rewards you hadn't cared about; you did well, without effort and
without heart, waiting all the time for the chance that would come
to abandon the daily job and deliver yourself over to your vocation.
So, all things considered, you had made a success of the career,
quite as far as you were prepared to give yourself to it.

Yes—awake now, looking down along your own cheeks while I
shut first one eye then the other, to see how different your profile
looks from the restricted range of each single vision—you half-

46

agreed. But you were holding back from giving yourself full credit. You do not shirk, ever, application of your natural scepticism to yourself. You were setting up in opposition, within you, the fact that after twenty years the vocation still had to take second place to the job. I read this from memory; in the self-absorbed, down-turned shaping of your lips. I am the one who quoted Camus to you years ago: *Whatever prevents you from doing your work has become your work.*

Fragments of old rationalizations came from me; from you. The recession which made it seem madness to give up a job with full social security in '74, the undoubted disadvantage of your known Left-wing associations if you were thinking of making a change at a time when there was a definite swing to the Right. And then I—was it you?—remarked how although one agonized over decisions one didn't really make them: time did. Time decides, I said. Look at us. You said, 'Well I'm not so sure. I've been a coward. About work. And about that too. There was a time...I don't know. The thing to do was to have made the break and married you. So I sometimes think.' Oh God, marriage...At least we didn't make a mess, I said. The two girls have had their home and their parents. We were lying with my lips touched by the hair of your breast, your hand curled over my shoulder, like two cats who have been wrestling luxuriously and slacken, holding in the attitude in which they have fallen apart the one in which they were lately locked. You said coldly—you are stern with yourself—'I'm not so proud of that.'

That's the cue. It was then exactly you found it possible, suddenly, to go on: 'My life...I don't know, it's a failure...and I'm between two girls at the moment.'

I had been lying there close to you, resting on the shore of your body attained. At these times you seem to take on physical functions for me; yours is the effort that makes us breathe. I had not known you were struggling, at least, to reach the moment when you could say this to me. Many times (you told me later) you had thought: now. But the words had not come. A decision such as this could not be acted upon, once in my presence. As we had just been saying: in the end, time takes care of it; it was easy, your mouth opened of itself and told me something that *in the act of telling* could be told because it no longer concerned me. It was something that happened to you; the time has come when things can happen to you without happening to me.

As you spoke, you became another being. I? I should never have guessed how it would be. I was seized—seized up—by the most alarming concentration of curiosity. I didn't know the need could be so terrible a desire. My life depended on your continuing to speak. I continued to lie in your arms. I moved my index finger in short, regular down-strokes on your chest, as one fills checks and pauses in a fatal discussion by shading scribbles on a desk-pad.

You told me about them. When you paused I didn't speak, showing you you must, forcing you to go on. The one is a colleague at your work. I think of her as the blonde—I don't ask you what they look like, I prefer to imagine, to pimp young beautiful women for you. But I did ask how old? About thirty-two or three.

You are not a sentimental man, the only person I've known who not merely ignores birthdays but even Christmas and the inescapably emotional event of a new calendar year. But as a matter of fact the other girl happens to be the female member of a couple your wife invited to a New Year's Day lunch. You had met the pair several times before, at other people's houses; your wife enjoys the social position having a rather distinguished husband earns her—an innocent pleasure you and I have been glad to think we could always grant her. You knew this girl 'felt something'; I suppose when in her company you told anecdotes with your self-deprecating humorous confidence among friends, and when your lucid dominance emerged from the confusion of political discussion. She has long dark hair—must have, because the nationality you mentioned was hers rules out any other colouring and makes any other style unlikely. At the New Year lunch your wife placed her on the host's right. 'I took her hand under the tablecloth.' You told me this, and doubling your chin, turning slightly, looked down at me, there on your breast, for the first time since you'd opened your eyes. It was a slightly comically-dismayed look. I know you so well; you can count on my understanding.

48

That's how it began, with her. The New Year is eight months
old. It's not easy to meet often; her husband's mother lives with
them and always wants to know where her son's young wife is
going. She is only twenty-five years old, this one. Really young,
you confessed, as at a gift you didn't ask for, accepted as of right
—and she's beautiful. Well (precision is one of your safeguards
against illusion) not so much beautiful as very—well—she's invit-
ing. A girl who can be overtaken by her appetites in an extraordinary way. And yet if you saw the husband, you'd think...the
husband is very young, too, good-looking. Quite intelligent. You
were helpless: 'She says she must stop seeing me and the next
week I find her sitting waiting for me in the place where I usually
grab lunch—we just go straight to some hotel.'

But it's the blonde one who made it necessary to speak. I understood that at once. She has a child she cannot give up. You couldn't
say how old—five or six?—which means you have seen it and feel
hostility towards it. She is the daughter of a woman who crawled
alive out of a pile of the dead in a concentration camp. Her father
was killed a year ago when terrorist gangs first began to gun down
embassy officials of countries whose connection with the gunmen's
cause is not easily apparent to those of us who read the newspaper
reports. He died in the street, in the lunch-hour of one of the
European capitals. While I remember some details so clearly I
could swear to them in a court of law, there must have been
moments when our unchanged position, my leg between yours,
your arm under my head, so impossible to believe, thundered
between my attention and your voice speaking. You were telling
the story with the detached enjoyment of drama that has always
made your stories striking; you were quite carried away by the
evil the blonde girl has had to survive before she could encounter
you. She does not love her husband, already they live in the
silence that overtakes marriages when people get old. The child
clings to her. It seems you and she discuss the future. You said to
her (you told me), 'How will you carry on living like this?'—And
of course that means you lie dreaming together of another way.—
She said to you, 'I'm one of millions.'

She attracts disaster, that one. I see it although I'll never see her.

She has the dreadful marks of a survivor. Like her mother. She doesn't want to go to an hotel. You told me that in your direct way. I don't know where it is you do find to take her.

Although we had not moved from one another's arms, already—how quickly one adapts to the unthinkable—I had the instinct to avoid the tiny brown nipple hidden in the hair of your breast. My hand knew already it would not seek you out again. The position in which we lay already belonged to the past.

I said to you:
I knew.
I go over the times when you didn't tell me. I knew you were thinking of another woman. Or women; in the great confessional of our early intimacy, an intimacy that, paradoxically, real daily familiarity (in marriage, for example) seals off, we talked about women. Your ability to seek out, attract, make love was discussed between us as a bounty. You would like to make love to every woman you find desirable. How many men have the energy to feel this, or the honesty to say it? You find very many women desirable —of all nationalities and races, a whole paint-selector card of colours—your delight in the variety of my sex delighted me, too. How many men really love women? Without any secret resentment, pity, or even disgust? Marvel at us, find every pathetic little physical differentiation, not only from their own bodies, but between one woman and the next, an experience that can't be forgone? And you took so much pleasure in me and in pleasing me. There was never any doubt, never mind that (being you) you were even able to tell me that sometimes immediately after you left me, so happy in your flesh and mind, you noticed a girl at the bus stop or near you in the tube train whom you felt deprived of. I laughed and kissed you when you could tell me these things. Wasn't I the one you wanted most? What more could I want? For the first and only time in my life I was free—free enough of tightly-nursed possession to understand this. Other women don't matter.

They didn't matter, so long as I did. When I say that I knew— I noticed what you didn't: you didn't walk beside me in the street, any more. Quite unconsciously, you would lead the way or fall behind, pausing to look in a shop-window or buy a newspaper as if you were alone. You sometimes looked blank when I referred to plans I had told you I had made or discussions I had related to you; you had heard but no longer listened. We were still together but you were not always with me. *I* wanted to speak, too. I wanted to say, have all the girls you can get; I have you. Don't feel any guilt towards me. I also wanted sometimes to forestall what perhaps you were waiting to tell me, by turning the proposition round, so to speak: so I said once, in a restaurant where we were having the kind of lunch with which neither of us would indulge other people—One day it will have to come to an end, I'll be the one to end it.

Your face looked very big. It became exposed and open to me. I had transfixed you there, among the old spotted silvery mirrors and the soft whiffs of exquisite food. Other pairs like us were shifting elbows closer across the tables, casting unfocused glances round this place that was the witness of their being together, slipping caresses along fingertips in the exchange of bread or a sauce-boat. I said: Come on. What's the matter?

You had stopped eating.

You said: 'You've just told me you're going to leave me.'

And then I made the inevitable retractions and explanations, backing away, away, both of us accepted them, beginning to drink wine and eat again, soothing, touching, backing away from what frightened us, the terrible opportunity I had offered you, my head on a plate, by my own hand, along with the pheasant with four sauces. I understand that now. You showed all the symptoms of extreme shock, not because you were afraid I would leave you but because you were frightened by the sudden opening to tell me what you were wanting to. In terms of power (the political but not personal nature of which we discuss often) you did not take your chance and there was a vacuum between us.

I remember other things. I see that although you didn't tell me anything about the two women who do not know of each other's existence for you, you could not resist referring to them obliquely or in passing. It's well known that when one is preoccupied or obsessed by someone there is this necessity to carry that person to the light of conversation. I am sure you don't remember, perhaps you'll even deny it—you mentioned the-blonde-one-at-work, she had pointed out to you some mistake that had been made or she had remarked intelligently or sardonically on some colleague's idiosyncrasies—'There's this quite clever girl, no, woman I should say, she noticed that old T—— really is beyond doing his job properly these days.' What you were thinking while you said this was that you had a meeting arranged with her for that afternoon, you were allowing yourself the secret joy of dwelling on the anticipation simply by the act of mentioning her existence to a third person—myself. And the other one—the graceful young dark one, I see her as very dark. Describing the usual family occasion we always have to endure apart, you told me how at this year's New Year lunch your brother-in-law became quite animated for once, even tried to be witty, in the company of a girl who arrived wearing some sort of exotic garment—the current craze for African or eastern dress. Your wife had to comfort her sister, whom wine had made jealous of the girl. So I knew about that one, too; you had told me, if I had been able to understand.

I knew.

There are many other things you might have been telling me that I would not hear. You said between the sixth floor and street level, looking at me as if I had asked for dispassionate opinion on some object I had bought, 'There is too much green stuff on your eyes.' I scrubbed at them, embarrassed as if I had appeared with some shameful bodily stain on my clothes. I looked at myself in shop-mirrors as we hurried along the street, I asked repeatedly, is it off, now? But you would not look at me again. You answered yes, concentrated ahead, in your turn perhaps embarrassed at having brought my attention to something I took so seriously, from you.

I know my skin has changed. In the sunlight of the street the schema of cosmetics does not emphasize contour and colour that is already there, it chalks a face that no longer exists. My real face is underneath and obvious, the skin drawn together so many countless times in the same concentration, hesitancy and determination, angers and anxieties, expanded in the same response of animation, affection and joy, that it has the intensity of expression that is simply the feature of the human face, and not the feature of a woman's. I am not old and ugly yet but you can see your death in my changing face. I am more agile and supple than you (when, from time to time, we have been able to spend a few days together we have competed with morning exercises on the floor of a hotel room) but in my slackened behind turned to you in the bathroom as I shower, in the sunburned wattle that webs between my thin jaw and my neck, you see the final softening of the flesh that is coming to you as a man one day, your death as a lover of women.

A HUNTING ACCIDENT

She met her photographer at the Kilimanjaro in Dar. To the new Missionaries—FAO and UNESCO representatives, Africa-desk journalists, arts and crafts teachers, Scandinavian documentary film-makers, Fanonist-Dumontist economist sons and daughters of dead or departed settler families—this means the hotel, not the mountain, and the monosyllable stands for Dar es Salaam. She was dossing down on the floor in the children's bedroom of a woman professor at the university so she had to wait for an invitation to his room. She saw at once that the photographer was not shy but (she hadn't heard of him) was probably somebody, and not on the look-out for women. It was the old story; she was accustomed to being taken notice of in a certain way. He sat with his pipe and old-fashioned oilcloth tobacco pouch in the bar, easy to find, and put aside his notebooks less to talk than to listen to her with deep attention; but it was not in that way. He quickly became her immediate purpose: she didn't show much guile and that was instinctively wise, because he saw that she had aban-doned the tactics that must serve a pretty girl so well, and she saw that he would not be able to resist honesty. When she had finished telling him something in her excited, indignant manner, he would think a long time, smiling at her, his lips pressed together, small-boned brown face fine-lined with the growing intensity of his expression, gazing green eyes darting side-glances away, as if he were laughing delightedly, privately, within, before he answered with his 'Why?' 'Would you?' 'I wonder.' He would not have the heart to reject her.

How exciting it was, to be received on such terms! In the sealed and carpeted hotel room he opened windows that were never meant to be opened and the heat-solid night into which she stretched her arm was even more airless. They agreed that velvet, foam-padded chairs and thick mattresses were Northern luxuries —Southern penances, and she talked of smooth tiles bare to soles, high walls punched free to the sea breeze by lattice. He stroked her sweaty hair away from her cheeks, and it was she who suggested they have a long shower together, he submitting to the old, sweet rites of sensuality with good grace.

It was she who brought him to Ratau's house in another African country. She tried out in her ear how other people might comment: She took him along with her from Tanzania. She thought how she might say to Ratau: Clive Nellen was in Dar, he so much wanted to photograph this country after I'd talked such a lot about it. Both were partly true. She had told him of the country she had been born in, daughter of the colonial Minister of Education, and her standing invitation to come back and stay with the youngest son of her father's old friend, the Paramount Chief. She had told him of the terracotta and bottle-green town built of red earth with hedges of Euphorbia, where the house was, and of the great tree near the house where the tribal court still met each day to decide disputes between citizens. He had come so far, it was a pity not to go farther—perhaps he had been intending to visit that country anyway; he did not discuss plans much. She brought her suitcase and duffle bag of books to his room and slept a last night with him in the hotel before they took an early plane together. They were met at the other end by one of Ratau's big cars with one of his cousins to drive them the hundred-and-twenty kilometres to the Chief's town. She watched her photographer's eyes flicking adjustment to the passing scrub and thought how when they were in bed (Ratau would at once understand they should be given a room together) she would be able to say to him: 'Didn't I tell you; that endless plain with a single hill peaked up here and there casting its single blue shadow—it's exactly the imaginary country old maps call "Land of Prester John" or "Kafferland".'

But they got to bed very late and, five or six people, some rather drunk, like noisy innocent children calling to one another from camp bed to sleeping bag, all slept at last before the fire in the living-room: Ratau had one of his house-parties. Friends from his university days in England and America, people he invited to stay when he was in various countries at various times, tended to turn up, and there were always also numerous members of the extended family of his father's three wives with a permanent claim on hospitality, taking it for granted that they would serve the household in some way while they were there. Ratau with his cajoling African laugh and his ruthless Cambridge accent had told everyone he was getting them all up to go on a hunting trip in the morning; at half-past six he was prodding at sleepers with his ready-laced boots and holding by the limp hand the little waxen-blonde Swedish potter from the crafts school in the village whom he had taken to the room he, as host, reserved to himself for the night. One of the distant relatives was behind him with a huge tin tray of coffee mugs and rusks. There was something stronger, Ratau called, for those who felt they had to keep out the morning cold. An old kitchen table stocked with brandy and gin and cane spirit stood permanently among the painted barrels of elephant ear and canvas chairs on the huge verandah that hooded the house. The guns were laid out there, too; he was giving orders to relatives summoned to act as bearers, breaking breeches, putting barrels to his left eye. 'Christie—tell me, your friend, what'sisname? He'll be one of the guns?' And she laughed, a shade disloyally, because Ratau was so attractive, so unselfconsciously male in his natural assumption of what she had been taught, at her progressive school, was the conditioned male role of killer. 'Shoot with his camera,' she said.

'Great. He'll see me get my eland today.'

'Ra-tau! Strictly prohibited! Didn't you tell me eland's pro-tected?'

'A chief's allowed one a year. My brother's turn last time, now I'm going to bag mine.' He lowered his voice, to tease or flirt: *I'll give you the skin to warm you in London.* She murmured, *Mean it?*

Always mean what I say, Christie.

The Swedish blonde was not around to hear. When Christine went out onto the gravel drive where a truck had come shaking up under the shouts of some relatives already mounted, she saw her, sitting on a white-washed boulder, yawn like a cat: she was cradling a reluctant toddler with the holy-family reverence Swedish girls display for black children. The photographer was moving about in his unnoticed way among people, his paraphernalia round his neck and bulging the pockets of his usual bush jacket and thin man's large shorts. He gave a hand with lowering the (broken) tail-gate of the truck so that people could climb in but he was not part of the shouting, squealing, laughing and innuendo that made these people who had got to know each other only the previous night feel they were such good friends. He smiled at her as he had before they were lovers; the breasts and thighs and backsides, knees, feet and arms comradely crowded together on the truck seemed to deny the reality of the physical presence he had lent her in a hotel room in Dar. He was certainly married; a passionate boy-and-girl love affair that was the basis of his privacy and whose transformation into domestic peace was the basis of his sympathetic detachment—she would take a bet on it, although she'd never asked him. She hoped, with the edge of defensiveness of one who is at fault, he wasn't sulking because she had said they'd go to the court under the tree and up to the Great Place where the chiefs were buried, this morning. She'd let herself and him be carried off on this hunting party; he might be thinking it was not the kind of thing he would enjoy, but was going along because it was the kind of thing *she* would enjoy—and she couldn't say, explain, excuse anything, lean a seducer's message against his breathing side in the press of the truck, because she was in the cab up front with Ratau driving and a young black woman, Yolisa, while he was in the open truck behind. She turned her head once and could just see him between jolts that brought others into her vision: little Ulla, the Swede, an old relative-retainer in an ancient balaclava, the huge, laughing engineer husband of Yolisa, a great round, neckless head like a Benin bronze bobbing on a vast chest —all with guns poking up between them. No of course her photographer wasn't sulking; he must be at least thirty-eight, not a young man of her own age who talked liberation and expected his girls to do whatever he decided.

Ratau drove with reckless authority through the quiet morning fires of his father's and forefathers' town and forded a river of goats on the road leading out of it. At several points in the open country a figure patched together from whatever the poor in rural areas can assemble against winter cold—scarecrow jackets, split patent shoes, a red knitted cap, a sack serving as a cape, a plaid blanket—rose from a culvert or appeared where cattle had tramped down the grass round a thorn tree. A man came towards the truck as to a rendezvous, hand raised in patient, trusted respect; Ratau landed in an applause of dust, shouting from the window to his bearers on the back, calling to the man on the road, who was, indeed, there by arrangement to report on the movement of game for the information of the hunt. Ratau turned and struck out accordingly across the plain to mopane forest, through mopane forest and out into the open again. In the freedom of driving without a road to follow—a progress as suddenly full of haphazard energy as a speedboat in rough water—the skill and comment and laughter of Ratau, the looming and lurching of gold-red trees, the din of the vehicle's clattering, grinding, chuntering metal bones, the people on the back of the truck seemed not to exist for the three in the cab. Once there was a thump on the roof and Ratau, roaring with laughter, slowed down a bit, but the timing with which he changed back and forth from lower to higher gear and the sureness with which he swung his way through wilderness inspired confidence that in his hands there was no danger to anyone, he would carry everyone through with him, even supposing there actually were to be a load of poor devils somewhere up behind.

In this din and euphoria a gun-shot was hardly more than a pop. It was the ragged scream borne away on the edge of the truck's noise and the battering of fists on the cab roof that made the three in the cab recognize the explosion. Yolisa gave a woman's answering cry to any cry, she clutched Christine's thigh. The truck came to a wild stop, Ratau's smooth black arm extended a hard, efficient barrier to prevent the women pitching to the windscreen. At some second's edge in the collision of seen, heard, felt, Christine saw a large object fall past the truck. She twisted her head to the rear window, feeling her neck snap against its stem; it was Yolisa's husband—: not there between the others. His big body flung aside. She imprisoned the black girl's clenched fists in her own; terror sucked her veins flat, she saw herself, them all, standing round this girl's husband, blood running its way, running, running to its ebb and no one with the skill or means to stop it. The helpless struggle of dreams held her in the truck; within that stasis she held fast to the girl to keep death off from her.

And then there was laughter. Shouts: of laughter. The door on the driver's side hung open where Ratau had jumped out. The big engineer was at the window on the passenger's side, signalling his wife to lower it, huffing and puffing, rubbing his right ear, being dusted down by others like a child who has taken a tumble. Christine and the young woman beside her whom she had met twenty-four hours before flung themselves together in a trembling embrace. Like lovers with a moment they cannot share, they hesitated before getting down from the cab. The husband put his arm round his wife as a man does at a party and grinned: 'Don't worry, you're not a widow yet.' She moved her shoulders and looked irritated. Ratau was teasing him, expertly therapeutic against shock. 'Good lord, man, the very sound of a shot and you think you're in the next world.' 'Well, I'm not so sure I'm here now— my ear's burning like hell.' 'Not a scratch to be seen, I assure you. You jumped out of your skin, that's all.' The sun, newly risen ruddy, thrust the gaiety of firelight through bronze, carmine, copper, brown and brass cinders of the dry mopane leaves and the static of goldened dust thrown up around them. The sleep that holds all forests was broken in upon by celebrating voices and unicorn bursts of laughter went bounding away into the solitude. Somebody got down a case of beer from the truck; it was cold as champagne. The cans were passed from mouth to mouth, calabash fashion. The gun-bearers in their blue overalls with bare black feet close together against the cold sandy earth, giggled with pleasure. They spoke no English and the little Swedish blonde was taking the opportunity to try and communicate through the few phrases of their language she had already learnt. This one and that gave versions of how the engineer had jumped, toppled, capered, dived from the truck. He slapped at his ear. 'I tell you, quite deaf on that side now. I felt the bullet sear the skin.' Someone crept up and shouted in the ear and he cried out; Ratau stood with commandingly outstretched arm, finger jabbing at him, conducting the general laughter.

She went up almost awkwardly to the photographer; he really

did act as if he were incredibly staid! It would give other people the wrong impression of the kind of man she chose. 'You were next to him, weren't you?'

He was lighting the pipe and continued to make small popping noises for a moment or two, those extraordinarily beautiful eyes that had excited her in Dar deeply translucent in three-quarter profile with their expression ellipsed as, at a certain angle, is the design that makes the pupil of a sea-glass marble. He smiled a little at her, round the pipe-stem. 'The bullet went between us—top of my head and his ear.'

Yes—the man she had brought to the party was the smallest and slightest there, when it came to build he didn't look much. 'Good God. What was it like?'

'Loud. He's lucky to be alive. If it'd been an inch to the left, it would have gone over the top of my head, if it'd been an inch to the right, it would've been in his brain.' This was in a low conversational voice no one else would have heard. All he said for the company in general was—more or less to Ratau—as the truck was manned again, 'Perhaps it would be a good idea if everyone checked the guns are unloaded.' Sensible but somehow the kind of dampening suggestion that would come from someone who didn't have quite the style to look danger gallantly in the eye the way this party did. What did he know about the handling of guns, anyway.

Ratau said, not unkindly, 'Don't worry, you'll come to no harm. Everything under control.'

The Swedish girl, already seated in the truck with the defensive smile of a terrified child, held to the hand, cold and tough as the feel of a tortoise's foot, of the old gun-bearer who had never before been touched by a white woman.

Twice the party caught up with three eland who threaded images swiftly into the mopane, a disappearing painted ribbon: the exquisite calligraphy of their broad flanks made them seem two-dimensional. Ratau never got within firing range. If he was disappointed, he was not the kind to show his guests the discourtesy of imposing this upon them; the truck bucked off in other directions, where other game had been reported by the scouts. In a natural park between mopane forests, a herd of red hartebeest grazed. They did not see the threat they did not know. The swaying truck did not fit the shape of any predator. The two women in the cab whispered to each other, 'Look! Look!' at the marvel of a pattern of life printed and yet moving glossy russet and cream, prehistory and yet alive (tails flicked, coats twitched at parasites, droppings fell elegantly); the herd progressed like a cloud or the outline of water, changing without breaking.

Ratau was out of the driver's seat, up onto the open truck. His bearers jumped down lightly knee-bent, spilled all round in a criss-cross of guns. He followed the English protocol; each of his guests must have the chance to drop a beast before he would take a shot himself. The air cracked and split over the truck. The ancient alert was marked by the single majestic signal of a horn-swept head. The herd left the way mercury runs, a mass without distinguishable components. Two hundred yards; and then stopped, the lovely masks facing the hunters. In low gear (beside Christine a relative smelling of clothing impregnated with wood-smoke was driving) the truck followed until within range. The guests fired again at their host's instruction. As a piece of rich cloth is grasped at one end and shaken, a shock-wave passed through the herd. They swung away and this time one could hear the wild hobble of their hooves. Some shapes lay on the ground where they had been; 'Five, we got five!' the engineer shouted. 'Six,' Ratau said, putting a hand on the shoulder of another of his friends. 'You aimed too low, old man; you've got him in the leg. Try for the neck now.' Christine and Yolisa had come down from the cab again. Christine had her hands on her hips, gazing. 'One's standing on its own under that tree, there! Look at that!' 'Albert's wounded him, his hind leg's gone.' 'Oh no!' 'Hop back in, there's a good girl.' She wanted to find the photographer and sit with him on the truck but the men, a herd themselves now, pushed past her unseeingly in their excitement and she had to do as Ratau said and get into the cab.

They rolled slowly across the plain towards the acacia under whose thin gauze of shade the markings of the red hartebeest showed cleanly. All eyes were fixed on it and it took the gaze as if waiting for them. It stood perfectly steady on three legs with the fourth, left hind, dangling snapped at the joint. There was only this disarticulation and a string of bright red blood to break the symmetry of the creature. 'A cow,' someone said; and someone else nodded. Ratau stood for encouragement beside the man whose prey it was. No one shuffled. The shot seemed released from the tension of all, and the beast collapsed, but the cry went up—'Still alive!' 'My God, finish it off, man!' Ulla and Yolisa covered their ears. 'Ratau, you do it!' But Ratau, the patient host, was instructing: 'Look, like this—you're point-blank, you can't miss—' Sweating, almost giggling with shame and rage at himself, the guest fired again into his beast that lay there panting, breathing still, looking at him, waiting for the death he owed her. Even that was not a clean shot, though a mortal one. Now she felt herself dying and with the last miracle of co-ordination she could muster drew back her head on the ground and gave a cow's cry, the familiar and gentle, pitiful moo of any clumsy dairy mother. It was as if it were discovered to be true that at midnight on Christmas Eve dumb beasts can speak their sufferings; no one had known that these wild beings could link the abattoir to the hunt, the slave to the free, in that humble bellow. Yolisa and Ulla fled to the cab. Christine stood with the second joint of her forefinger clasped between her bared teeth; she was not thinking of the animal; how horrible this was, he would be thinking, he who had not taken any part, active or vicarious, who had been brought along when what he wanted was to be looking at the Victorian monuments where Ratau's ancestors lay, and watching the council of elders administering the law in the shade of the assembly place, finding sermons in those gravestones and tongues in that tree.

Suddenly she saw he had leapt down from the truck and was walking quickly over to the dying beast. The shorts and veldskoen boots made his small, hard, thin legs look like an ill-nourished schoolboy's, the weighed-down pockets of the bush jacket and the leather straps of two cameras yoked him. He was walking right into the gaze they all decently turned away from. He went straight up to the beast and, down on one knee, began to photograph it again and again, close-up, gazing through the camera, with the camera, into the last moments of life passing in its open eyes. His face was absolutely intent on the techniques he was employing; there was a deep line she had never seen before, drawn down either side of his mouth from the sucked-in nostrils. He placed filters over his lens, removed them. He took his time. The beast tried to open its mouth once more but there was no sound, only a bubble of blood. Its eye (now the head had lolled completely into profile, he could see only one) settled on him almost restfully, the faculty of vision bringing him into focus, then fading, as he himself looked steadily into it with his camera.

He came back to the truck, where Ratau was explaining the reactions of a herd after some of the animals have dropped. She murmured, 'It's still moving'—from afar, the body twitched slackly like a kicked bundle.

'No,' he said. 'She's gone.' He was writing (a date, some figures) in his curling notebook that smelt of tobacco.

The final bag was nineteen—twelve red hartebeest and seven blesbok, most dropped stone-dead with single shots from the host's gun. The eland were not seen again. Yolisa sat in the cab, not looking out, and said, 'All I want is to get back and see if my baby's all right.' Another truck arrived, finding its way in the wake of the first as if along signposted city streets, and relatives collected and flung up the carcasses with tremendous admiration and glee, making a party-cloakroom pile of pelts and blood.

The women said they wouldn't touch any of the meat Ratau promised them that night: 'You'll see, red hartebeest is the best eating of any game.' When evening came, and beneath the mantel photograph of the old Paramount Chief with his looped watch-chain, Homburg hat and leopard skin, the fire spread the delicious incense of burning tambuti wood among the red-wine drinkers, and the hunger of the open air was pleasurable as lust, all ate from the belly-shaped enamel pots a one-eyed relative brought round. 'Should have been hung first'—Ratau referred Christine to the English cuisine they both knew—'But here, with us, nobody wants to wait.' In the kitchen there was feasting, and out in the yard still more people were cooking on a communal open fire. Christine had a lot to drink. She kept an eye on the curiously childlike figure in the old shorts and bush jacket, she was conscious of the smell of his pipe always somewhere in the room, despite the tambuti scent, despite the loudness of the rock music, and she hoped they would get somewhere to sleep alone tonight. She evaded the men who had been dancing with her and found him. 'Are you mad with me?'

He was chatting quietly to an old black man who was trying his tobacco in a home-made pipe. 'Why?'

'Well that's all right then.' She had an urge to kiss passionately that wise-monkey, aesthete's face, to put her hands up under the old khaki clothes and beat her fists at the breast there. He smiled at her affectionately in his appreciation of the old man: she read, 'Go off and enjoy yourself.'

But it was not till the morning that she held his message in her hand. By the time she got up and picked her way among the sleepers on the living-room floor, he had gone with the railway bus that paused, palsied by its sonorous diesel engine, to take on passengers and their small livestock for the capital. He had left a note for her, enclosing another to thank Ratau for his hospitality. Both smelled of proximity to the oilcloth tobacco pouch. 'You'll be glad to know I saw the sun rise from the Great Place today. It's all you said. You've also said there's nowhere else to stay but a Holiday Inn. I'll be based there. For about a week until the 25-6th, I should think. If you should come down, you'll find me queued up at the help-yourself before the curry-and-rice trough, lunchtime.'

She walked through the garden, where butterflies of blossom were alighted on the bauhinia trees and blood-tendoned bones and tufts of hide, dragged from the yard overnight by dogs, littered the oval of ashen winter grass. Flies blundered at her face. Out in the road dust was luxurious as cream underfoot; under the huge tree old men were assembled and a disaffected citizen or two, hat and stick marking formality, awaited the outcome of a long harangue. She hung about, not too near, as if she had only to be able to understand, that's all, and the speaker would have something to say, for her.

FOR DEAR LIFE

Swaying along in the howdah of her belly I make procession up steep streets. The drumming of her heart exalts me; I do not know the multitudes. With my thumb-hookah I pass among them unseen and unseeing behind the dancing scarlet brocades of her blood. From time to time I am lurched to rest. Habituation to the motion causes me to move: as if the hidden presence raps testy impatience. They place their hands to read a sign from where there is no cognition of their existence.

A wall-eyed twenty-five-year-old Arab with a knitted cap jumps back into the trench in a cheerful bound. Others clamber stockily, with the dazed open mouth of labourers and the scowl of sweat. Their work-clothes are cast-off pin-stripe pants brought in rumpled bundles from Tunis and Algiers. Closely modelled to their heads and growing low, straight across their foreheads, their kind of hair is a foreign headgear by which they see themselves known even if they do not speak their soft, guttural, prophet's tongue. One has gold in his mouth, the family fortune crammed into crooked teeth. Another is emaciated as a beggar or wise man, big feet in earth-sculpted boots the only horizontal as his arms fly up with the pick. Eyes starred like clowns' with floury dust look up from the ditch just at the level where the distortion of the female body lifts a tent of skirt to show the female thighs. She's a young one. Mending roads and laying sewage pipes through the French resort over more than a year, they have seen her walking with the man who wanted her, in pursuit, hunting her even while he and she walked side by side, with his gilt-buckled waist, his handbag manacled to his wrist, his snakeskin-snug shirt showing sportsman shoulders, his satyr's curly red hair, thin on top, creeping down the back of his neck and breast-bone, glinting after her along with his eyes and smile.

Like the other women in this country, she was not for them. She did not nod at them then and the mouth parted now as she's approaching is not the beginning of the greeting she has for the postman or any village crone. She's simply panting under her eight-month burden: in there, another foreman, overseer, *patron* like the one who will come by any minute to make sure they are not idling.

Here—feel it?
Concentrate on the drained Cappuccino cups spittled with chocolate-flecked foam. The boom of the juke box someone's set in motion seems to be preventing...as if it were a matter of hearing, through the palm!
Give me your hand—
A small-change clink as silver bracelets on the older woman's wrist move with volition surrendered.
There. *There.* Lower down, that's it—now you *must* be able to.
But was it not always something impossible to detect from outside... So long ago: tapping, plucking (yes, that was much more the way it was)—plucking at one's flesh from within as fingers fidget pleating cloth. If I were the one, now, you were inside, I should feel you. You would be unmistakable. You would be unlike the children he had or the children I had. You are a girl because he had no girl. His daughter with his stiff-legged walk (heron-legs, I used to say) and my bottom (bob-tail, he used to say) and his oval nails and fine white skin behind the ears. You can crack your knee and ankle joints. Tea-leaves tinsel the grey of your irises. Like him, like me. You have our face; when we used to see ourselves as a couple in the mirror of a lift that was carrying us clandestinely.

The doctor says they suck their thumbs in the womb. Sucks its thumb!
As if the doctor were a colleague the young husband confirms with a nod, gazing assessingly at the majestic mound that rises out of the level of water in the bath. Like many people without a profession he has a magazine-article amateur's claim to knowledge in many.
My boy's been shown what life is all about from when he

wasn't more than an infant in arms. No sweets, look at the state my teeth are in. You'll finish school whatever happens. That's all very fine, earning enough to buy yourself a third-hand Porsche 'C' '59 at nineteen but at thirty-four you find yourself selling TV sets on commission, during a recession. No running around the summer streets, twelve years old and ought to be asleep at night. No chasing girls, catching them, squeezing their little breasts on the dark porch of the old church before it was pulled down. Steer clear of married women who keep you in bed, spoilt bitches, while their husbands get on in the world and buy the Panther West-winds de Ville, modelled after the Bugatti Royal, best car ever made, Onassis had one, and Purdey guns, gold cigarette lighters, camera equipment, boats with every comfort (bar, sauna)—you could even live on board, for instance if you couldn't get a rent-controlled flat. Great lover, but the silk shirts and real kid boots from Italy don't last long when you're hanging around bars look-ing for work and all you get offered is the dirty jobs the Arabs are here to do. No smoking, either; bad enough that your mother and I mess up our lungs, 20 per cent reduction of life-expectancy, they say. You'll have more sense or I'll know why. You'll be lucky. Women love red hair, a well-known sign of virility. You'll fly first class with free champagne. You'll fill in forms: 'Company Direc-tor'. *You'll do as I say.* If you aren't given Coca-Cola to taste, you won't miss it.

Feel—my belly's so hard. I'm like a rock.

She does not know the name, but she is thinking of a geode halved, in a shop window; a cave of crystals, a star cracked open. In there, curved as a bean, the wonder of her body blindly gazes.

How long to go?

It is an old woman's form of greeting. Her stiff dog stands with his front paws on the kitchen window and watches the heads below that come into view and pass. He lifts his nose slightly, as at a recollection, when a boy clatters from the baker's to the hotel with a head-dress of loaves. Beside the dog the crone looks down at a dome under which sandalled feet show, like the cardboard feet of one of those anthropomorphic balloon toys, and above which a bright, smooth face smiles up at her with the kindly patronage of the young.

It can't be long: for her. Every day, when she and the dog manage to get as far as the front step to sit down in a series of very slow movements in the sun at noon, you can count the breaths left.

He will stand behind a desk in his Immigration Officer's uniform and stamp how long they can stay and when they must go. He will drive up in his big car that rises and sinks on its soft springs in the dust as a bird settles upon water, and not bother to get out, giving orders through the window to the one among them who understands the language a little better than the others.

No one will know who you are; not even you.

Only we, who are forgetting each other, will know who you never were.

Even possibilities pass.

I don't cry and I don't bleed.

My daughter wanted for nothing. I bought a Hammond organ on instalments because she's so musical. (Since she was a little thing.) She could have gone to a good convent although we're not religious. Right, she wanted a car, I got her a car and she drove around without a licence: I warned her. The boys were crazy for her; her mother talked to her. She looked like eighteen at fourteen with that figure and that beautiful curly red hair. You don't see anything like it, usually it all comes out of a bottle. I won't have her making herself cheap. She could go to study at the university or take up beauty culture. There's money in that. If anyone lays a finger on her—

The emaciated ditch-digger weeps sometimes as he digs. It is on Mondays that the sight occurs among them, when he is suffering from the drink their religion forbids. His brother has committed

suicide in Marseilles knowing the sickness of the genitals he had
was punishment for offending Allah by going with a white whore.

It is summer round the empty house in the fields the family left
two generations ago. They can't go back, except to picnic like
tourists who bring their cheese and wine and ashamed little caches
of toilet paper onto anyone's property. There's no electricity and
there's water only in a well. They spray the old vines once a year,
and once a year come for the grapes. Cows from neighbouring
farms stare from the grass with their calves.

I lean in the solid shadow of the mother's body, against her flanks.

To those who have already lived, an empty house is unimagin-
able. They build it only out of what has been placed by the hands
of man: from the bricks that enclose space to the rugs put down
and curtains drawn there, once—how can there be *nobody*? The
ornamental wooden valance that is breaking away from the eaves
is the blows of the grandfather who nailed it. The Virgin with a
cake-doily gilt lace halo under glass is the bedroom faith of a
grandmother. An old newspaper is the eyes of one who read it.

When I vacate this first place I'll leave behind the place that
was all places. I'll leave behind nothing. There will be *nothing*—
for I'm taking all with me, I'm taking it on...all, all, everything.
In my swollen sex, obscene for my size, in my newly-pressed-into-
shape cranium containing the seed-pearls of my brain cells, in my
minute hands creased as bank-notes or immigration papers. Head
down, shoving, driven, meeting violence with violence, casting
myself out like Jonah from the heaving host whale, bursting lungs
that haven't breathed yet, swimming for dear life...

I don't see them covering their eyes in secret, I don't hear them
wailing: It will all be gone through again!

Behind me, the torn membranes of my moorings.

Hauled from the deep where there is no light for sight I
find eyes. The ancient Mediterranean sun smithereens against me
like a joyous glass dashed to the ground.

Ta mère fit un pet foireux et tu naquis de sa colique.

I begin again.

TOWN AND COUNTRY LOVERS
One

Dr Franz-Josef von Leinsdorf is a geologist absorbed in his work; wrapped up in it, as the saying goes—year after year the experience of this work enfolds him, swaddling him away from the landscapes, the cities and the people, wherever he lives: Peru, New Zealand, the United States. He's always been like that, his mother could confirm from their native Austria. There, even as a handsome small boy he presented only his profile to her: turned away to his bits of rock and stone. His few relaxations have not changed much since then. An occasional skiing trip, listening to music, reading poetry—Rainer Maria Rilke once stayed in his grandmother's hunting lodge in the forests of Styria and the boy was introduced to Rilke's poems while very young.

Layer upon layer, country after country, wherever his work takes him—and now he has been almost seven years in Africa. First the Côte d'Ivoire, and for the past five years, South Africa. The shortage of skilled manpower brought about his recruitment here. He has no interest in the politics of the countries he works in. His private preoccupation-within-the-preoccupation of his work has been research into underground water-courses, but the mining company that employs him in a senior though not executive capacity is interested only in mineral discovery. So he is much out in the field—which is the veld, here—seeking new gold, copper, platinum and uranium deposits. When he is at home—on this particular job, in this particular country, this city—he lives in a two-roomed flat in a suburban block with a landscaped garden, and does his shopping at a supermarket conveniently across the street. He is not married—yet. That is how his colleagues, and the typists and secretaries at the mining company's head office, would define his situation. Both men and women would describe him as a good-looking man, in a foreign way, with the lower half of the face dark and middle-aged (his mouth is thin and curving, and no matter how close-shaven his beard shows like fine shot embedded in the skin round mouth and chin) and the upper half contradictorily young, with deep-set eyes (some would say grey, some black), thick eyelashes and brows. A tangled gaze: through which concentration and gleaming thoughtfulness perhaps appear as fire and languor. It is this that the women in the office mean when they remark he's not unattractive. Although the gaze seems to promise, he has never invited any one of them to go out with him. There is the general assumption he probably has a girl who's been picked for him, he's bespoken by one of his own kind, back home in Europe where he comes from. Many of these well-educated Europeans have no intention of becoming permanent immigrants; neither the remnant of white colonial life nor idealistic involvement with Black Africa appeals to them.

One advantage, at least, of living in underdeveloped or half-developed countries is that flats are serviced. All Dr von Leinsdorf has to do for himself is buy his own supplies and cook an evening meal if he doesn't want to go to a restaurant. It is simply a matter of dropping in to the supermarket on his way from his car to his flat after work in the afternoon. He wheels a trolley up and down the shelves, and his simple needs are presented to him in the form of tins, packages, plastic-wrapped meat, cheeses, fruit and vegetables, tubes, bottles... At the cashiers' counters where customers must converge and queue there are racks of small items uncategorized, for last-minute purchase. Here, as the coloured girl cashier punches the adding machine, he picks up cigarettes and perhaps a packet of salted nuts or a bar of nougat. Or razor-blades, when he remembers he's running short. One evening in winter he saw that the cardboard display was empty of the brand of blades he preferred, and he drew the cashier's attention to this. These young coloured girls are usually pretty unhelpful, taking money and punching their machines in a manner that asserts with the time-serving obstinacy of the half-literate the limit of any responsibility towards customers, but this one ran an alert glance over the selection of razor-blades, apologized that she was not allowed to leave her post, and said she would see that the stock was replenished 'next time'. A day or two later she recognized him, gravely, as he took his turn before her counter—'I ahssed them, but it's out of stock. You can't get it. I did ahss about it.' He said this didn't matter. 'When it comes in, I can keep a few packets for you.' He thanked her.

He was away with the prospectors the whole of the next week. He arrived back in town just before nightfall on Friday, and was on his way from car to flat with his arms full of briefcase, suitcase and canvas bags when someone stopped him by standing timidly in his path. He was about to dodge round unseeingly on the crowded pavement but she spoke. 'We got the blades in now. I didn't see you in the shop this week, but I kept some for when you come. So...'

He recognized her. He had never seen her standing before, and she was wearing a coat. She was rather small and finely-made, for one of them. The coat was skimpy but no big backside jutted. The cold brought an apricot-graining of warm colour to her cheek-bones, beneath which a very small face was quite delicately hollowed, and the skin was smooth, the subdued satiny colour of certain yellow wood. That crêpey hair, but worn drawn back flat and in a little knot pushed into one of the cheap wool chignons that (he recognized also) hung in the miscellany of small goods along with the razor-blades, at the supermarket. He said thanks, he was in a hurry, he'd only just got back from a trip—shifting the burdens he carried, to demonstrate. 'Oh shame.' She acknowledged his load. 'But if you want I can run in and get it for you quickly. If you want.'

He saw at once it was perfectly clear that all the girl meant was that she would go back to the supermarket, buy the blades and bring the packet to him there where he stood, on the pavement. And it seemed that it was this certainty that made him say, in the kindly tone of assumption used for an obliging underling, 'I live just across there—*Atlantis*—that flat building. Could you drop them by, for me—number seven-hundred-and-eighteen, seventh floor—'

She had not before been inside one of these big flat buildings near where she worked. She lived a bus- and train-ride away to the West of the city, but this side of the black townships, in a township for people her tint. There was a pool with ferns, not plastic, and even a little waterfall pumped electrically over rocks, in the entrance of the building *Atlantis*; she didn't wait for the lift

marked GOODS but took the one meant for whites and a white
woman with one of those sausage-dogs on a lead got in with her
but did not pay her any attention. The corridors leading to the
flats were nicely glassed-in, not draughty.

He wondered if he should give her a twenty-cent piece for her
trouble—ten cents would be right for a black; but she said, 'Oh
no—please, here—' standing outside his open door and awkwardly
pushing back at his hand the change from the money he'd given
her for the razor-blades. She was smiling, for the first time, in
the dignity of refusing a tip. It was difficult to know how to treat
these people, in this country; to know what they expected. In
spite of her embarrassing refusal of the coin, she stood there,
completely unassuming, fists thrust down the pockets of her cheap
coat against the cold she'd come in from, rather pretty thin legs
neatly aligned, knee to knee, ankle to ankle.

'Would you like a cup of coffee or something?'

He couldn't very well take her into his study-cum-living-room
and offer her a drink. She followed him to his kitchen, but at the
sight of her pulling out the single chair to drink her cup of coffee
at the kitchen table, he said, 'No—bring it in here—' and led the
way into the big room where, among his books and his papers, his
files of scientific correspondence (and the cigar boxes of stamps
from the envelopes) his racks of records, his specimens of minerals
and rocks, he lived alone.

It was no trouble to her; she saved him the trips to the supermarket and brought him his groceries two or three times a week.
All he had to do was to leave a list and the key under the doormat,
and she would come up in her lunch-hour to collect them, return-
ing to put his supplies in the flat after work. Sometimes he was
home and sometimes not. He bought a box of chocolates and
left it, with a note, for her to find; and that was acceptable,
apparently, as a gratuity.

Her eyes went over everything in the flat although her body tried
to conceal its sense of being out of place by remaining as still as
possible, holding its contours in the chair offered her as a stranger's

coat is set aside and remains exactly as left until the owner takes it up to go. 'You collect?'

'Well, these are specimens—connected with my work.'

'My brother used to collect. Miniatures. With brandy and whisky and that, in them. From all over. Different countries.'

The second time she watched him grinding coffee for the cup he had offered her she said, 'You always do that? Always when you make coffee?'

'But of course. Is it no good, for you? Do I make it too strong?'

'Oh it's just I'm not used to it. We buy it ready—you know, it's in a bottle, you just add a bit to the milk or water.'

He laughed, instructive: 'That's not coffee, that's a synthetic flavouring. In my country we drink only real coffee, fresh, from the beans—you smell how good it is as it's being ground?'

She was stopped by the caretaker and asked what she wanted in the building? Heavy with the *bona fides* of groceries clutched to her body, she said she was working at number 718, on the seventh floor. The caretaker did not tell her not to use the whites' lift; after all, she was not black; her family was very light-skinned.

There was the item 'grey button for trousers' on one of his shopping lists. She said as she unpacked the supermarket carrier, 'Give me the pants, so long, then,' and sat on his sofa that was always gritty with fragments of pipe tobacco, sewing in and out through the four holes of the button with firm, fluent movements of the right hand, gestures supplying the articulacy missing from her talk. She had a little yokel's, peasant's (he thought of it) gap between her two front teeth when she smiled that he didn't much like, but, face ellipsed to three-quarter angle, eyes cast down in concentration with soft lips almost closed, this didn't matter. He said, watching her sew, 'You're a good girl'; and touched her.

She remade the bed every late afternoon when they left it and she dressed again before she went home. After a week there was a day when late afternoon became evening, and they were still in the bed.

'Can't you stay the night?'

'My mother,' she said.

'Phone her. Make an excuse.' He was a foreigner. He had been in the country five years, but he didn't understand that people don't usually have telephones in their houses, where she lived. She got up to dress. He didn't want that tender body to go out in the night cold and kept hindering her with the interruption of his hands; saying nothing. Before she put on her coat, when the body had already disappeared, he spoke. 'But you must make some arrangement.'

'Oh my mother!' Her face opened to fear and vacancy he could not read.

He was not entirely convinced the woman would think of her daughter as some pure and unsullied virgin... 'Why?'

The girl said, 'S'e'll be scared. S'e'll be scared we get caught.'

'Don't tell her anything. Say I'm employing you.' In this country he was working in now there were generally rooms on the roofs of flat buildings for tenants' servants.

She said: 'That's what I told the caretaker.'

She ground fresh coffee beans every time he wanted a cup while he was working at night. She never attempted to cook anything until she had watched in silence while he did it the way he liked, and she learned to reproduce exactly the simple dishes he preferred. She handled his pieces of rock and stone, at first admiring the colours—'It'd make a beautiful ring or a necklace, ay.' Then he showed her the striations, the formation of each piece, and explained what each was, and how, in the long life of the earth, it had been formed. He named the mineral it yielded, and what that was used for. He worked at his papers, writing, writing, every night, so it did not matter that they could not go out together to public places. On Sundays she got into his car in the basement garage and they drove to the country and picnicked away up in the Magaliesberg, where there was no one. He read or poked about among the rocks; they climbed together, to the mountain pools. He taught her to swim. She had never seen the sea. She squealed and shrieked in the water, showing the gap between her teeth, as—it crossed his mind—she must do when among her own people. Occasionally he had to go out to dinner at the houses of colleagues from the mining company; she sewed and listened to the radio in the flat and he found her in the bed, warm and already asleep, by the time he came in. He made his way into her body without speaking; she made him welcome without a word. Once he put on evening dress for a dinner at his country's consulate; watching him brush one or two fallen hairs from the shoulders of the dark jacket that sat so well on him, she saw a huge room, all chandeliers and people dancing some dance from a costume film—stately, hand-to-hand. She supposed he was going to fetch, in her place in the car, a partner for the evening. They never kissed when either left the flat; he said, suddenly, kindly, pausing as he picked up cigarettes and keys, 'Don't be lonely ' And added, 'Wouldn't you like to visit your family sometimes, when I have to go out?'

He had told her he was going home to his mother in the forests and mountains of his country near the Italian border (he showed her on the map) after Christmas. She had not told him how her mother, not knowing there was any other variety, assumed he was a medical doctor, so she had talked to her about the doctor's children and the doctor's wife who was a very kind lady, glad to have someone who could help out in the surgery as well as the flat.

She remarked wonderingly on his ability to work until midnight or later, after a day at work. She was so tired when she came home from her cash register at the supermarket that once dinner was eaten she could scarcely keep awake. He explained in a way she could understand that while the work she did was repetitive, undemanding of any real response from her intelligence, requiring little mental or physical effort and therefore unrewarding, his work was his greatest interest, it taxed his mental capacities to their limit, exercised all his concentration, and rewarded him constantly as much with the excitement of a problem presented as with the satisfaction of a problem solved. He said later, putting away his papers, speaking out of a silence: 'Have you done other kinds of work?' She said, 'I was in a clothing factory before. Sportbeau shirts; you know? But the pay's better in the shop.'

Of course. Being a conscientious newspaper-reader in every country he lived in, he was aware that it was only recently that the retail consumer trade in this one had been allowed to employ coloureds as shop assistants; even punching a cash register represented advancement. With the continuing shortage of semi-skilled whites a girl like this might be able to edge a little farther into the white-collar category. He began to teach her to type. He was aware that her English was poor, even though, as a foreigner, in his ears her pronunciation did not offend, nor categorize her as it would in those of someone of his education whose mother tongue was English. He corrected her grammatical mistakes but missed the less obvious ones because of his own sometimes exotic English usage—she continued to use the singular pronoun 'it' when what was required was the plural 'they'. Because he was a foreigner (although so clever, as she saw) she was less inhibited than she might have been by the words she knew she misspelled in her typing. While she sat at the typewriter she thought how one day she would type notes for him, as well as making coffee the way he liked it, and taking him inside her body without saying anything, and sitting (even if only through the empty streets of quiet Sundays) beside him in his car, like a wife.

On a summer night near Christmas—he had already bought and hidden a slightly showy but nevertheless good watch he thought she would like—there was a knocking at the door that brought her out of the bathroom and him to his feet, at his work-table. No one ever came to the flat at night; he had no friends intimate enough to drop in without warning. The summons was an imperious banging that did not pause and clearly would not stop until the door was opened.

She stood in the open bathroom doorway gazing at him across the passage into the living-room; her bare feet and shoulders were free of a big bath-towel. She said nothing, did not even whisper. The flat seemed to shake with the strong unhurried blows.

He made as if to go to the door, at last, but now she ran and clutched him by both arms. She shook her head wildly; her lips drew back but her teeth were clenched, she didn't speak. She pulled him into the bedroom, snatched some clothes from the clean laundry laid out on the bed and got into the wall-cupboard, thrusting the key at his hand. Although his arms and calves felt weakly cold he was horrified, distastefully embarrassed at the sight of her pressed back crouching there under his suits and coat; it was horrible and ridiculous. *Come out!* he whispered. *No! Come out!* She hissed: *Where? Where can I go?*

Never mind! Get out of there!

He put out his hand to grasp her. At bay, she said with all the force of her terrible whisper, baring the gap in her teeth: *I'll throw myself out the window.*

She forced the key into his hand like the handle of a knife. He closed the door on her face and drove the key home in the lock, then dropped it among coins in his trouser pocket.

He unslotted the chain that was looped across the flat door. He turned the serrated knob of the Yale lock. The three policemen, two in plain clothes, stood there without impatience although they had been banging on the door for several minutes. The big dark one with an elaborate moustache held out in a hand wearing a plaited gilt ring some sort of identity card.

Dr von Leinsdorf said quietly, the blood coming strangely back to legs and arms, 'What is it?'

The sergeant told him they knew there was a coloured girl in the flat. They had had information; 'I been watching this flat three months, I know.'

'I am alone here.' Dr von Leinsdorf did not raise his voice.

'I know, I know who is here. Come—' And the sergeant and his two assistants went into the living-room, the kitchen, the bathroom (the sergeant picked up a bottle of after-shave cologne, seemed to study the French label) and the bedroom. The assistants removed the clean laundry that was laid upon the bed and then turned back the bedding, carrying the sheets over to be examined by the sergeant under the lamp. They talked to one another in Afrikaans, which the Doctor did not understand. The sergeant himself looked under the bed, and lifted the long curtains at the window. The wall cupboard was of the kind that has no knobs; he saw that it was locked and began to ask in Afrikaans, then politely changed to English, 'Give us the key.'

Dr von Leinsdorf said, 'I'm sorry, I left it at my office—I always lock and take my keys with me in the mornings.'

'It's no good, man, you better give me the key.'

He smiled a little, reasonably. 'It's on my office desk.'

The assistants produced a screwdriver and he watched while they inserted it where the cupboard doors met, gave it quick, firm but not forceful leverage. He heard the lock give.

She had been naked, it was true, when they knocked. But now she was wearing a long-sleeved T-shirt with an appliquéd butter-fly motif on one breast, and a pair of jeans. Her feet were still bare; she had managed, by feel, in the dark, to get into some of the clothing she had snatched from the bed, but she had no shoes. She had perhaps been weeping behind the cupboard door (her cheeks looked stained) but now her face was sullen and she was breathing heavily, her diaphragm contracting and expanding exaggeratedly and her breasts pushing against the cloth. It made her appear angry; it might simply have been that she was half-suffocated in the cupboard and needed oxygen. She did not look at Dr von Leinsdorf. She would not reply to the sergeant's questions.

They were taken to the police station where they were at once separated and in turn led for examination by the district surgeon. The man's underwear was taken away and examined, as the sheets had been, for signs of his seed. When the girl was undressed, it was discovered that beneath her jeans she was wearing a pair of men's briefs with his name on the neatly-sewn laundry tag; in her haste, she had taken the wrong garment to her hiding-place.

Now she cried, standing there before the district surgeon in a man's underwear.

He courteously pretended not to notice. He handed briefs, jeans and T-shirt round the door, and motioned her to lie on a white-sheeted high table where he placed her legs apart, resting in stir-rups, and put into her where the other had made his way so warmly a cold hard instrument that expanded wider and wider. Her thighs and knees trembled uncontrollably while the doctor looked into her and touched her deep inside with more hard instruments, carrying wafers of gauze.

When she came out of the examining room back to the charge

office, Dr von Leinsdorf was not there; they must have taken him somewhere else. She spent what was left of the night in a cell, as he must be doing; but early in the morning she was released and taken home to her mother's house in the coloured township by a white man who explained he was the clerk of the lawyer who had been engaged for her by Dr von Leinsdorf. Dr von Leinsdorf, the clerk said, had also been bailed out that morning. He did not say when, or if she would see him again.

A statement made by the girl to the police was handed in to Court when she and the man appeared to meet charges of contravening the Immorality Act in a Johannesburg flat on the night of — December, 19—. *I lived with the white man in his flat. He had intercourse with me sometimes. He gave me tablets to take to prevent me becoming pregnant.*

Interviewed by the Sunday papers, the girl said, 'I'm sorry for the sadness brought to my mother.' She said she was one of nine children of a female laundry worker. She had left school in Standard Three because there was no money at home for gym clothes or a school blazer. She had worked as a machinist in a factory and a cashier in a supermarket. Dr von Leinsdorf taught her to type his notes.

Dr Franz-Josef von Leinsdorf, described as the grandson of a baroness, a cultured man engaged in international mineralogical research, said he accepted social distinctions between people but didn't think they should be legally imposed. 'Even in my own country it's difficult for a person from a higher class to marry one from a lower class.'

The two accused gave no evidence. They did not greet or speak to each other in Court. The Defence argued that the sergeant's evidence that they had been living together as man and wife was hearsay. (The woman with the dachshund, the caretaker?) The magistrate acquitted them because the State failed to prove carnal intercourse had taken place on the night of — December, 19—.

The girl's mother was quoted, with photograph, in the Sunday papers: 'I won't let my daughter work as a servant for a white man again.'

Two

The farm children play together when they are small; but once the white children go away to school they soon don't play together any more, even in the holidays. Although most of the black children get some sort of schooling, they drop every year farther behind the grades passed by the white children; the childish vocabulary, the child's exploration of the adventurous possibilities of dam, koppies, mealie lands and veld—there comes a time when the white children have surpassed these with the vocabulary of boarding-school and the possibilities of inter-school sports matches and the kind of adventures seen at the cinema. This usefully coincides with the age of twelve or thirteen; so that by the time early adolescence is reached, the black children are making, along with the bodily changes common to all, an easy transition to adult forms of address, beginning to call their old playmates *missus* and *baasie*—little master.

The trouble was Paulus Eysendyck did not seem to realize that Thebedi was now simply one of the crowd of farm children down at the kraal, recognizable in his sisters' old clothes. The first Christmas holidays after he had gone to boarding-school he brought home for Thebedi a painted box he had made in his wood-work class. He had to give it to her secretly because he had nothing for the other children at the kraal. And she gave him, before he went back to school, a bracelet she had made of thin brass wire and the grey-and-white beans of the castor-oil crop his father cultivated. (When they used to play together, she was the one who had taught Paulus how to make clay oxen for their toy spans.) There was a craze, even in the *platteland* towns like the one where he was at school, for boys to wear elephant-hair and other bracelets beside their watch-straps; his was admired, friends asked him to get similar ones for them. He said the natives made them on his father's farm and he would try.

When he was fifteen, six feet tall, and tramping round at school dances with the girls from the 'sister' school in the same town;

when he had learnt how to tease and flirt and fondle quite intimately these girls who were the daughters of prosperous farmers
like his father; when he had even met one who, at a wedding he
had attended with his parents on a nearby farm, had let him do
with her in a locked storeroom what people did when they made
love—when he was as far from his childhood as all this, he still
brought home from a shop in town a red plastic belt and gilt hoop
ear-rings for the black girl, Thebedi. She told her father the
missus had given these to her as a reward for some work she had
done—it was true she sometimes was called to help out in the
farmhouse. She told the girls in the kraal that she had a sweetheart
nobody knew about, far away, away on another farm, and they
giggled, and teased, and admired her. There was a boy in the kraal
called Njabulo who said he wished he could have bought her a
belt and ear-rings.

When the farmer's son was home for the holidays she wandered
far from the kraal and her companions. He went for walks alone.
They had not arranged this; it was an urge each followed independently. He knew it was she, from a long way off. She knew that
his dog would not bark at her. Down at the dried-up river-bed
where five or six years ago the children had caught a leguaan one
great day—a creature that combined ideally the size and ferocious
aspect of the crocodile with the harmlessness of the lizard—they
squatted side by side on the earth bank. He told her traveller's
tales: about school, about the punishments at school, particularly,
exaggerating both their nature and his indifference to them. He
told her about the town of Middleburg, which she had never seen.
She had nothing to tell but she prompted with many questions,
like any good listener. While he talked he twisted and tugged at
the roots of white stinkwood and Cape willow trees that looped
out of the eroded earth around them. It had always been a good
spot for children's games, down there hidden by the mesh of old,
ant-eaten trees held in place by vigorous ones, wild asparagus
bushing up between the trunks, and here and there prickly-pear
cactus sunken-skinned and bristly, like an old man's face, keeping
alive sapless until the next rainy season. She punctured the dry
hide of a prickly-pear again and again with a sharp stick while she

listened. She laughed a lot at what he told her, sometimes dropping her face on her knees, sharing amusement with the cool shady earth beneath her bare feet. She put on her pair of shoes—white sandals, thickly Blanco-ed against the farm dust—when he was on the farm, but these were taken off and laid aside, at the river-bed.

One summer afternoon when there was water flowing there and it was very hot she waded in as they used to do when they were children, her dress bunched modestly and tucked into the legs of her pants. The schoolgirls he went swimming with at dams or pools on neighbouring farms wore bikinis but the sight of their dazzling bellies and thighs in the sunlight had never made him feel what he felt now, when the girl came up the bank and sat beside him, the drops of water beading off her dark legs the only points of light in the earth-smelling, deep shade. They were not afraid of one another, they had known one another always; he did with her what he had done that time in the storeroom at the wedding, and this time it was so lovely, so lovely, he was surprised... and she was surprised by it, too—he could see in her dark face that was part of the shade, with her big dark eyes, shiny as soft water, watching him attentively: as she had when they used to huddle over their teams of mud oxen, as she had when he told her about detention weekends at school.

They went to the river-bed often through those summer holidays. They met just before the light went, as it does quite quickly, and each returned home with the dark—she to her mother's hut, he to the farmhouse—in time for the evening meal. He did not tell her about school or town any more. She did not ask questions any longer. He told her, each time, when they would meet again. Once or twice it was very early in the morning; the lowing of the cows being driven to graze came to them where they lay, dividing them with unspoken recognition of the sound read in their two pairs of eyes, opening so close to each other.

He was a popular boy at school. He was in the second, then the first soccer team. The head girl of the 'sister' school was said to have a crush on him; he didn't particularly like her, but there was a pretty blonde who put up her long hair into a kind of doughnut with a black ribbon round it, whom he took to see films when the schoolboys and girls had a free Saturday afternoon. He had been driving tractors and other farm vehicles since he was ten years old, and as soon as he was eighteen he got a driver's licence and in the holidays, this last year of his school life, he took neighbours' daughters to dances and to the drive-in cinema that had just opened twenty kilometres from the farm. His sisters were married, by then; his parents often left him in charge of the farm over the weekend while they visited the young wives and grandchildren.

When Thebedi saw the farmer and his wife drive away on a Saturday afternoon, the boot of their Mercedes filled with fresh-killed poultry and vegetables from the garden that it was part of her father's work to tend, she knew that she must come not to the river-bed but up to the house. The house was an old one, thick-walled, dark against the heat. The kitchen was its lively thorough-fare, with servants, food supplies, begging cats and dogs, pots boiling over, washing being damped for ironing, and the big deep-freeze the missus had ordered from town, bearing a crocheted mat and a vase of plastic irises. But the dining-room with the bulging-legged heavy table was shut up in its rich, old smell of soup and tomato sauce. The sitting-room curtains were drawn and the T.V. set silent. The door of the parents' bedroom was locked and the empty rooms where the girls had slept had sheets of plastic spread over the beds. It was in one of these that she and the farmer's son stayed together whole nights—almost: she had to get away before the house servants, who knew her, came in at dawn. There was a risk someone would discover her or traces of her presence if he took her to his own bedroom, although she had looked into it many times when she was helping out in the house and knew well, there, the row of silver cups he had won at school.

When she was eighteen and the farmer's son nineteen and work-ing with his father on the farm before entering a veterinary college, the young man Njabulo asked her father for her. Njabulo's parents met with hers and the money he was to pay in place of the cows it is customary to give a prospective bride's parents was settled upon. He had no cows to offer; he was a labourer on the Eysendyck farm, like her father. A bright youngster; old Eysen-dyck had taught him brick-laying and was using him for odd jobs

in construction, around the place. She did not tell the farmer's son
that her parents had arranged for her to marry. She did not tell
him, either, before he left for his first term at the veterinary
college, that she thought she was going to have a baby. Two
months after her marriage to Njabulo, she gave birth to a daughter.
There was no disgrace in that; among her people it is customary for
a young man to make sure, before marriage, that the chosen girl is
not barren, and Njabulo had made love to her then. But the infant
was very light and did not quickly grow darker as most African
babies do. Already at birth there was on its head a quantity of
straight, fine floss, like that which carries the seeds of certain weeds
in the veld. The unfocused eyes it opened were grey flecked with
yellow. Njabulo was the matt, opaque coffee-grounds colour that
has always been called black; the colour of Thebedi's legs on
which beaded water looked oyster-shell blue, the same colour as
Thebedi's face, where the black eyes, with their interested gaze
and clear whites, were so dominant.

Njabulo made no complaint. Out of his farm labourer's earn-
ings he bought from the Indian store a cellophane-windowed pack
containing a pink plastic bath, six napkins, a card of safety pins,
a knitted jacket, cap and bootees, a dress, and a tin of Johnson's
Baby Powder, for Thebedi's baby.

When it was two weeks old Paulus Eysendyck arrived home
from the veterinary college for the holidays. He drank a glass of
fresh, still-warm milk in the childhood familiarity of his mother's
kitchen and heard her discussing with the old house-servant
where they could get a reliable substitute to help out now that the
girl Thebedi had had a baby. For the first time since he was a
small boy he came right into the kraal. It was eleven o'clock in
the morning. The men were at work in the lands. He looked about
him, urgently; the women turned away, each not wanting to be
the one approached to point out where Thebedi lived. Thebedi
appeared, coming slowly from the hut Njabulo had built in white
man's style, with a tin chimney, and a proper window with glass
panes set in straight as walls made of unfired bricks would allow.
She greeted him with hands brought together and a token movement representing the respectful bob with which she was accus-

tomed to acknowledge she was in the presence of his father or mother. He lowered his head under the doorway of her home and went in. He said, 'I want to see. Show me.'

She had taken the bundle off her back before she came out into the light to face him. She moved between the iron bedstead made up with Njabulo's checked blankets and the small wooden table where the pink plastic bath stood among food and kitchen pots, and picked up the bundle from the snugly-blanketed grocer's box where it lay. The infant was asleep; she revealed the closed, pale, plump tiny face, with a bubble of spit at the corner of the mouth, the spidery pink hands stirring. She took off the woollen cap and the straight fine hair flew up after it in static electricity, showing gilded strands here and there. He said nothing. She was watching him as she had done when they were little, and the gang of children had trodden down a crop in their games or transgressed in some other way for which he, as the farmer's son, the white one among them, must intercede with the farmer. She disturbed the sleeping face by scratching or tickling gently at a cheek with one finger, and slowly the eyes opened, saw nothing, were still asleep, and then, awake, no longer narrowed, looked out at them, grey with yellowish flecks, his own hazel eyes.

He struggled for a moment with a grimace of tears, anger and self-pity. She could not put out her hand to him. He said, 'You haven't been near the house with it?'

She shook her head.

'Never?'

Again she shook her head.

'Don't take it out. Stay inside. Can't you take it away somewhere. You must give it to someone—'

She moved to the door with him.

He said, 'I'll see what I will do. I don't know.' And then he said: 'I feel like killing myself.'

Her eyes began to glow, to thicken with tears. For a moment there was the feeling between them that used to come when they were alone down at the river-bed.

He walked out.

Two days later, when his mother and father had left the farm for the day, he appeared again. The women were away on the lands, weeding, as they were employed to do as casual labour in summer; only the very old remained, propped up on the ground outside the huts in the flies and the sun. Thebedi did not ask him in. The child had not been well; it had diarrhoea. He asked where its food was. She said, 'The milk comes from me.' He went into Njabulo's house, where the child lay; she did not follow but stayed outside the door and watched without seeing an old crone who had lost her mind, talking to herself, talking to the fowls who ignored her.

She thought she heard small grunts from the hut, the kind of infant grunt that indicates a full stomach, a deep sleep. After a time, long or short she did not know, he came out and walked away with plodding stride (his father's gait) out of sight, towards his father's house.

The baby was not fed during the night and although she kept telling Njabulo it was sleeping, he saw for himself in the morning that it was dead. He comforted her with words and caresses. She did not cry but simply sat, staring at the door. Her hands were cold as dead chickens' feet to his touch.

Njabulo buried the little baby where farm workers were buried, in the place in the veld the farmer had given them. Some of the mounds had been left to weather away unmarked, others were covered with stones and a few had fallen wooden crosses. He was going to make a cross but before it was finished the police came and dug up the grave and took away the dead baby: someone—one of the other labourers? their women?—had reported that the baby was almost white, that, strong and healthy, it had died suddenly after a visit by the farmer's son. Pathological tests on the infant corpse showed intestinal damage not always consistent with death by natural causes.

Thebedi went for the first time to the country town where Paulus had been to school, to give evidence at the preparatory examination into the charge of murder brought against him. She cried hysterically in the witness box, saying yes, yes (the gilt hoop ear-rings swung in her ears), she saw the accused pouring liquid into the baby's mouth. She said he had threatened to shoot her if she told anyone.

More than a year went by before, in that same town, the case was brought to trial. She came to Court with a new-born baby on her back. She wore gilt hoop ear-rings; she was calm; she said she had not seen what the white man did in the house.

Paulus Eysendyck said he had visited the hut but had not poisoned the child.

The Defence did not contest that there had been a love relationship between the accused and the girl, or that intercourse had taken place, but submitted there was no proof that the child was the accused's.

The judge told the accused there was strong suspicion against him but not enough proof that he had committed the crime. The Court could not accept the girl's evidence because it was clear she had committed perjury either at this trial or at the preparatory examination. There was the suggestion in the mind of the Court that she might be an accomplice in the crime; but, again, insufficient proof.

The judge commended the honourable behaviour of the husband (sitting in court in a brown-and-yellow-quartered golf cap bought for Sundays) who had not rejected his wife and had 'even provided clothes for the unfortunate infant out of his slender means'.

The verdict on the accused was 'not guilty'.

The young white man refused to accept the congratulations of press and public and left the Court with his mother's raincoat shielding his face from photographers. His father said to the press, 'I will try and carry on as best I can to hold up my head in the district.'

Interviewed by the Sunday papers, who spelled her name in a variety of ways, the black girl, speaking in her own language, was quoted beneath her photograph: 'It was a thing of our childhood, we don't see each other any more.'

A MAD ONE

The telephone rang beside the bed in the middle of the night and she woke struggling across her husband's body to grab the receiver. Their movements under the bedclothes might have denoted mating or fighting; the fact was that even in sleep she was alert to the humiliation of hearing him answer the telephone without teeth in his mouth. Plastic grin there under his pillow, old age in the dark. He fumbled and thrashed to find it, hampered by her weight.

But she had reached the phone first, thank god. Heart a drumroll of apprehension, she could hear nothing. A nuisance call? As wildly as he searched out the teeth, she dug from her ears the wax plugs of her infirmity: sleep worn so thin it could not withstand the smallest night creak or dawn cheep. Lying across his chest, she heard the charming daytime voice of one for whom the sun shines at midnight like glitter on patent leather; for whom morning, beginning as indifferently with a sundowner of gin as with cereal, brings no day appropriately defined by work. 'Is Leif Harder there—?'

A kick of her elbow against her support, his chest, conveyed to him at once what this was—a call from his dead brother's wife.

Her again. The cold, chemical-tasting grin had clamped itself into his tender mouth; a freed arm turned on the light as his wife Elena went through the useless and exasperating ritual of her obstinate conviction that that woman must be made to face reality (even in the bloody small hours).

'He is, yes. In bed, fast asleep. So's everyone in the house. D'you know what time it is?'

'Oh Christ! Give here,' he said.

'Well I can tell you—' Elena strained to see the dial of his watch, resting on the book he'd fallen asleep over.

'Give here!'

'Ten-past three.'

He heard the chortling, confessing laughter, although his wife still held the receiver.

'—Yes. *In the morning.*'

The charming laughter was in his ear as he gained command of the telephone; that woman found herself infinitely entertaining. When she was in a good mood—or had had a lot to drink?—her verdict was that other people were too stuffy and inhibited to appreciate her. 'Leif—good god, you were getting your beauty sleep. Of course. I'm terribly sorry. I never go to bed early, I didn't realize...and you know how I hate clocks...'

'Well what is it, Ruthie. Won't it wait till morning, then.' The diminutive his poor brother had added to her name persisted, in the family, the more firmly attached as it became less and less appropriate to her personality.

'Oh you are cross. Leif, I just thought you might know where Vic has gone.'

'Vic? What you mean, gone? Isn't he living with his friends in some old house? D'you mean he's been back with you?'

'No, no, wait. Wait, Leif—'

He lifted a hand, let it drop on the pillow; Elena rolled to her own hollow in the bed. She stopped listening; now and then the static of that woman's voice reached her in a rising cadence. She knew the course of the monologue her husband was punctuating, she had heard it, or one like it, many times. It ended as it had many times. That woman wept with sudden rage; Leif could not be roused out of the weary calm that ruined the drama in which she had cast him as her male lead, for the course of the telephone call.

'She's put down the receiver on me.'

His wife forced laughter, to appreciate irony. 'That's right. First wakes us up at three in the morning, then bangs down the phone once she's talking to you.'

He got out of bed, stumbling a little with the imbalance of sleep in his limbs. She knew he would take the opportunity to go and relieve his bladder once he'd been wakened. 'Quarrels with her son six months ago, they haven't spoken since, and now she hears he's taken up with some girl, so she expects *me* to get a *court order*—'

'Oh tell me tomorrow.'

While he was in the lavatory, the telephone rang. Only once;

before it could make her cringe a second time she leaned again over his side of the bed and unplugged the thing. She turned out the light. He made his way clumsily to bed in the dark; he knew she would not answer if he wanted to go back to roost chatting.

He slept (each always thought the other slept instantly) while she lay bound and gagged in dreams of drowning, earthquakes, and car crashes to which she could not be summoned with a call to save her children because she was tethered to her conscious mind by the wire of the disconnected telephone.

In the kitchen after breakfast she found an opening by asking Agnes if there was still a shoulder of lamb left in the freezer? A relative from overseas was coming to dinner. '—So tired I can't remember. Master Vic's mother woke us up in the middle of the night.' The black servant's point of reference, for the family, was through its siblings.

Although Agnes had worked for the household for seventeen years and no doubt knew as much as its members knew about each other, she also knew there were some things she was told and must be prepared to talk about, and others she would never be told and could not admit to knowing. 'Again? Same like last week!'

'Three o'clock. Then I couldn't sleep...worrying about Matthew. Did he get the clothes I sent. They never bother to write. How can you sleep if the phone disturbs you at that time.'

'What is it wrong now?'

'Oh always the same. Trouble. Fighting with Master Vic.'

'Money or what?'

'Well, maybe. He's found a girl he wants to marry, but until he's twenty-one the mother has the money his father left for him.'

'That's nice he get marry! I think that's nice?'

'She wants to stop it, she wants Master to get the police—'

The head, wearing an old beret instead of the maid's neat cap provided, bobbed up from the great backside and legs bent over the freezer. Flesh was built into the hollow of the knees like blobs of clay on a sculptor's maquette. 'Really! That woman!'

But amused rather than appalled.

Three or four years ago (one survives, almost forgets) the same thing happened to the black woman as to her mistress—a school-girl daughter discovered to be pregnant. Agnes wailed, writhed on the kitchen floor and had to be comforted, while she herself, of course, could turn her attention to practical measures without the indulgence of hysterics. The resolution of the calamity made of it not the same thing at all...? An abortion was arranged for her daughter, while Agnes's daughter produced a small boy, Kgomotso, adored by his grandmother.

From time to time she felt this urge to go and tell Agnes, to put before Agnes something quite intimate.

Friends offered the trials and burdens of other families. The instinct was to divert, perhaps, out of boredom or lack of interest; to conquer-by-countering one problem about which no one knew what to say by relating another for which no one had the answer. The Lebigs' twenty-year-old son, chronic bed-wetter and stammerer, couldn't have any sort of normal relation with a girl; with all their money, nothing could be done. Brenda Graham's mother was eighty-seven, suffering from senile paranoia, and they couldn't afford to send her to an institution. The Bianchis had a problem child from *his* first marriage who stole from supermarkets. Alice and Benjamin Napier's son, that good-looking blond boy, was caught with drugs and got four years—imagine, they sit in that lovely house of theirs, full of books and pictures, and think of him in prison; Alice has begun to drink. Johnny Chesterfield's wife, who ran away with a Portuguese barman, was destitute and he'd had to take her back although he wanted to marry the young journalist who was expecting his baby. Clare Patch was in an alcoholics' home again, her lover left her and she tried to set fire to his car; her sister was paying. Archie Stein had taken an overdose— exactly like Ruthie Harder, holding everyone to ransom for a life he didn't have the first idea how to manage.

The conversation was always discovered to have gone a long way from this, its subject, and to have returned full circle in every sense: no one was any better off. The identification offered was with a general helplessness and distress. Time to change the subject.

'Why doesn't Vic do something? Why can't *Vic* take over? She's his mother.'

'Now you're just talking for talking's sake. If you're bored with what concerns your mother and me, then say so.'

'—But she is his mother. I *know* she didn't bring him up, I know he can't stand her. I know all that. It's not the point. If Ma went to pieces, she drank or something, or tried to kill herself—'

She smiled, not because this eventuality was inconceivable but at hearing herself called Ma: it was at Cambridge on a scholarship that the boy had learned to drop the colonial 'mom', recognize the refined vulgarity of middle-class 'mummy', and take on the usage that only the upper class dared adopt from the working class.

'It's a matter of self-preservation, idiot. —How thick can you be! Poor devil of a Vic, he's only just got away with his sanity. He's just beginning to put himself painfully together with the help of this little girl.' Whenever she came home for a family meal, the daughter (married now but still childless) fell into an irritability with her brother based on the habit of childhood resentment.

'If Ma made a damn nuisance of herself I'd consider it my—'

(And if you were chronic bed-wetter, stammerer, couldn't have any normal relation, got four years, I'd consider it my—) Now his mother giggled aloud at herself, as 'Ma', making a little grimace of besotted complicity for the benefit of the Scandinavian relative, out in Africa on a trip, in whose honour the lamb had been roasted. But both the terminological quaintness, and the significance of the mother's infatuation with a son were lost on this old third or fourth cousin (Leif's side). Her English was not good enough; she was not sure what everyone was talking about so passionately and uneasily, anyway.

The boy persisted. 'But surely there are friends? Can't anyone help? Didn't she used to run around a lot with the Braithwaites and that crowd—'

'Good god, don't you remember, there was that awful business

at the hotel on the way to Cape Town, they haven't had anything
to do with her for years.'

'It must be horribly lonely.'

'We all *know* it's lonely. But if you can't get on with anybody
...people can take just so much, and that's all. We *know* it's
horribly lonely.'

'Damn it all, Ma, whose fault is that?'

'Nobody's saying it's anyone's fault, idiot. You can't reduce life
to childish tit-for-tat.'

'—What's that got to do with it? There isn't a subject under the
sun you couldn't turn into an opportunity to get at me. Lucky
Matthew, out of reach in his ashram. India's just far enough away
from this family.'

'Leave each other alone...' Their mother's tone of voice separated the brother and sister as her hands had when they were
children.

'—Isn't even really family, is she—good god, she and Uncle
Jody were divorced for years before he died! I'm sick of this poor-
widow ploy. What's Dad got to do with her troubles at this stage?
I'm sick of hearing about it every time I come home.'

'Oh yes. Easy to say.'

'Separated. Never divorced. He couldn't divorce. She threatened to kill Vic and herself.'

'Just tell her *to go to hell*. Why shouldn't you?'

'Because then she will.'

There was silence. It was broken by the slow voice of the
Swedish relative—'Please, have you perhaps got a glass of beer?
I don't like so much to eat this meat without a little beer.'

'Leif!' The husband always neglected to see that guests' drinks
were replenished.

'All right, all right. I'm getting it.'

While his father was out of the room the son insisted: 'Why
doesn't he just tell Ruthie to go to hell.'

'It'd make more sense to get her to a psychiatrist again.'

The son-in-law took the can of beer from his father-in-law and
made the gesture of taking over hostly obligations, opening it and
pouring it, the head controlled, into a beer-mug for the Swedish

lady. The daughter helped her to more cucumber salad. 'Why not yoga? I see there's something called a transcendental meditation centre started up. She ought to be sent there for a few months to get herself straight.'

The son poured some more wine for himself; then quickly filled his mother's glass again. Bottle in hand, not offering it to anyone else, he was tall, above the table. '—Let her cut her wrists. What do you do but postpone it?'

Elena felt the wine unbind her tongue and knew she must not allow herself to speak. And heard herself: 'What would happen if she didn't have Leif? What if Leif dies? I'd have to take it on, wouldn't I? What could I do? —Wouldn't I? There'd be no end of it. It'd fall on me.'

'How old is the woman now, for god's sake—she must be well into middle age. Surely if you got together with friends—must be *somebody* left, if you spoke to Vic seriously about his mother, after all—you could send her to live at the coast somewhere—'

'Ruthie—cannot—live—alone.' The father confined himself to the facts.

'Exactly. She has to have someone to listen to her.'

'What does it matter how old. You talk as if this were a normal person. Such people never mature. That's the point.'

'*Exactly*. Of all the crazy ideas. Aren't you *helpful*. She'd be back in a week, phoning Dad from some expensive hotel in the middle of the night.'

Now the old Swedish cousin suddenly understood. 'Oh I know how is it. With crazy persons. I am sorry for this family.'

Elena was embarrassed that this should have turned out to be the night they had decided to ask her for dinner. 'Oh Margareta, I apologize. What a way to entertain you. It all blew up again early this morning, you see. It's awful to impose this sort of boring—'

'We have such a thing in our family, in Östersund, when I was young. A mad one. The sister of Birgit—you know who that was, Leif? The mother of your father's second wife—she was crazy. Even when we were at school. And then she was married with the doctor's son and she ran away one time with his little brother—he was not more than seventeen years, I think. It was a big scandal. In that little town of ours, you can think on it! Always she came back to the family. Someone found her here or here and brought her back. She just got more crazy. I remember at last she used to spend all day in the cemetery, singing and putting flowers on all the graves. Every grave with her flowers. Even in the rain.'

Everyone was aware of the rudeness of having ignored the guest through dinner. The daughter, with her easy, unfeeling sociability, began to chat. 'Daddy, who was your father's second wife? Was she the one with the frizzy blonde hair in that photo taken in front of a wooden house? You used to say that was Erster-whatever-you-call-it.'

The son gave his mother wine as if it were life-blood she was in need of, and she called out—'Margareta, what did they do?'

The Swedish cousin had finished her food with neat enjoyment and accomplishment. 'Excuse me?'

'What did they do about her?'

The replete guest sat alert and at ease. 'Oh my father, he had to buy flowers each day. Each day he bought flowers. It cost much. And in winter it was not possible. My aunt used to make them, flowers of paper, you know.'

Elena did not often drink more than a glass of wine. She recognized well the symptoms of having drunk four or five; she would swagger for attention and laughter, talk to dominate the table. Nothing to be done about it. 'D'you hear that? Oh... (a wail of envy) they bought her flowers every day. They just went out and supplied the mad one with flowers, winter and summer——'

Everybody laughed; the Swedish cousin looked pleased, again not quite understanding but feeling herself to have contributed to a change of mood round the table. The son and son-in-law began to talk about a fuel-saving device people were buying for their cars. The daughter and her father, who was carving the shoulder of lamb for second helpings, discussed exactly what the Swedish 'tundra' meant. Elena, hearing her own voice louder than anyone else's, hit upon the brilliant idea of asking cousin Margareta how to pickle cucumbers the way the Scandinavians did it. There was some real Aalborg Leif found to give her with the coffee. She said that in Sweden aquavit was served as an aperitif and never as a liqueur, but accepted a glass.

In bed, Elena unplugged the telephone. While her husband was in the bathroom she suddenly connected it again; then pulled it out once more. She had just regained her side of the bed when he came in. She saw his glance observe that the telephone was disconnected. He hesitated, she thought, for the flick of the glance, then got into bed. She drank a full glass of water to offset the dry mouth that, because of the wine, might make her wakeful in the middle of the night. She lay on the tomb of the bed and thought of flowers. They were minute, star-shaped Northern flowers she had never seen alive, of a kind that come up where there has been snow; dried and dyed, in shops. Wine unbound much more than her tongue. A huge dismay slowly ruptured inside her quiet body. She was dropsical with it. Waters had broken, but not in parturition. She said a banner in her dark: *we don't know how to live, do we*. But not aloud. She didn't want him to turn and protest, he would already have taken out the teeth.

YOU NAME IT

S he has never questioned who her father was. Why should she? Why should I tell her?

And yet there are times—times when we are getting on each other's nerves as only women and their daughters can— I have such a flash of irritable impulse: You are not...I had—

I think I am stopped only by not knowing how to put it most sensationally. How to make her stand in her tracks as she's walking out the door with her boy for a 'drive' (= to make love in the car; that old synonym). To see her face, when she's been keeping it turned away from me half-listening while I talk to her, suddenly wrenched round. Or when I feel it's time to leave the room because I've been monopolizing the conversation among her friends and they are boring, anyway. How to break in: with a name, a statement.

I took a piece of cane waste from the flotsam and wrote on the wet sand:

Arno   Arno Arkanius

The cane was hollow, blackened by fire, and the sharp broken end was a bold quill; it incised letters cleanly.

She couldn't read. There were hundreds of tiny flies feeding on the rotting seaweed among the cane and she sat turning her hands from the wrist in their swarm. She enjoyed the weightless feel of the insects or admired their gratifying response to her presence, I don't know which, she was still too young to speak. While the other children were at kindergarten we walked every morning on that beach which could not be called deserted because there never had been anyone there to be counted absent, except the island women who came to dig for bait. Their black legs in the water and their hunched backsides in old sacks had the profile of wading birds. They did not look up and I never learnt so much as a greeting in their language. We made the staggering progress of a woman with a small child who cannot speak, has no sense of time, and to whom the dirt rim of the sea's bath-tub is something to grasp while the blown-grass swells of the Indian Ocean, the porpoises jack-knifing in and out the water, the spice off the spray and the cliffs and hollows of Strelitzia palms in flower, are outside awareness.

Yes—it was a kind of paradise, I suppose, the kind open to people who drill for oil or man air bases or negotiate the world's purchase of sugar or coconut oil. I was born on one and married onto another and met the man who made her with me when transferred to this one. Our names were no guide to our place of habitation. They were the names of different origins all over Europe, cross-pollinated in the sports and games and parties in colonies and islands to which none was native. I don't know exactly what he was; Swedes sometimes have Latin names, but he came from a cotton pasha family that had had to leave Egypt, went to school in Lausanne, and was in the trade section of the consulate of one of the European countries who were losing their colonies but still setting the price for what they bought from them. He stayed two years before he was posted somewhere else—it was the usual tour of duty.

When the baby was born it looked, the first time, exactly like him but it was all right: never again. When I saw it I was filled with love—not for the infant but for him. It was six months since he had made love to me on the stripped bed with his suitcases standing by ready for the airport. Once again I yearned wildly. The emotion brought milk to my breasts. A few warm drops welled from the nipples, like tears. The nurses were pleased. My husband, delighted to have a girl child after two boys, tender and jocular in his happiness: *Now I'm prepared to let her off any more. Duty nobly done, dynasty assured. Unfortunately my daughter's as ugly as her brothers but give her time, we'll marry her yet.*

It was true that she became like her brothers as babies; a baby like all other babies, drooling saliva down the back of my dress when I held her the way she yelled to be held with her face over my shoulder, going slowly red in the face with silent concentration when she sat relieving herself, clutching my skirt when she wanted to pull herself up from the floor, holding her breath to the point of suffocation, in temper; looking so beautiful in her nightly drunken stupor with her bottle slack in her hand that my husband would take guests into the bedroom to gaze at her.

Her father never saw her. We wrote to each other all through the months before she was born; he had tried to persuade an island doctor whom he knew to give me an abortion, but there was his position at the consulate to consider, and my husband's position in the company. We were afraid the story would leak out. Whereas there was nothing exceptionable about my having a third child.

He dared not keep a photograph of her in case his wife came upon it. By the time the child was nearly a year old he was on home leave—apparently Europe was selected as home—and we wrote more seldom but I could take advantage of Christmas to send a card showing a colour photograph of the family with the baby girl smiling in the middle. He wrote that she seemed to have a very large mouth?—was that just the photograph? His wife had remarked on it, too.

I remember that I walked around the house carrying the letter and stared—nothing but sea, out there, nothing to be got from it but the sound of its endlessly long yawn and the tough glitter of its midday skin, and I went into the bedroom and lay down on the floor in the darkened room with my legs open, spread-eagled on my own cross, waiting for him. I cried to relieve myself, rolled on-to my face and let the saliva run out of my open mouth upon the dust and lint of the carpet, like the baby. After a long time I began to hear the sea again, and saw, under the bed in which I slept with my husband, a coin and his lost espadrilles with the backs flattened to the soles by the way he always pushed his feet into them. When the island girl who helped with the children brought them up from the beach I met the baby with resentment for not being prettier, but she did not notice; like everything and everyone around me, she was living a life where this did not matter; and there was no other. There was no other, for me.

I had boasted to him of the men who pursued me, including an ambassador, very distinguished and old enough to be my father. But now I wrote that I wanted a tidal wave to engulf the whole stupid life of the island; I did not tell him that I was flirting, and getting drunk at parties, and quarrelling with my husband because he said I neglected the children. To tell the truth these things didn't seem to me to be real—they were what I did to pass the time. Sometimes I wrote and said I was going to get divorced and take the baby and live alone. He replied that he was terrified 'something would happen to me'. We wrote as if these two sets of circumstances—his fearing for me, and my deciding to get divorced—had come about independently of each other, and of us. He instructed me not to write again until he could send a suitable new address—the two years were up once more, he was being re-posted once more, and we didn't want my letters lying round the consulate for prying hands to forward. At this time my husband had taken it upon himself to send for his mother to supervise the children and the atmosphere in the house was one of blinding, deafening, obsessive antagonism: the tidal wave that I had wished on myself. I did not even realize that a month had passed without any new address coming. Now I did leave my husband; I went without the baby, without any child. The old reason for leaving was submerged under the fierce rows and recriminations that swept through the house so that the servants went about subdued, eyes lowered, before all that was laid waste while furniture and flower vases stood as usual and the outside man went on skimming the swimming pool with a net scoop. Once my husband had suddenly shouted I ought to have been taken to see a doctor, that's what he should have done—it was only since the last baby was born that I'd behaved like this, I'd changed with the birth of that baby, he wished the bloody baby had never been born!

He, who was so besotted with her that she has been the over-indulged darling of the family, all her life. And I, not having the impulse then, at all, to fling back at him a name, a statement to stand out on his face harder than the print of any hand.

It was true that pretty terrible things could happen to me. I took a job as an air hostess on the inter-island service. I had no training for any occupation. The ceiling of the old DC 3s' flight was in the blanket of humidity and turbulence that rose from lovely mountains covered in tropical forest and lowland plantations of silky green cane. The cabins were not pressurized and I went up and down the aisles collecting paper bags of vomit. He must have heard about it, I'm sure, in his new posting to another set of island paradises, this time in the West Indies. Because of course, carrying my burdens along the aisles, I met the astonished eyes of passengers who knew me as the wife of the such-and-such company's man. The ambassador who had once brought me a box of real lilies of the valley from Europe (orchids were nothing, they grew wild on the island) stared at me from his seat, unsure whether or not to recognize me, although, like most women who have good taste in clothes and who for some reason have to put on a vulgarly provocative outfit, a waitress's dirndl or an air hostess's Courrèges, I knew my looks had been sexually charged by the uniform. Another passenger and his wife, to whom I made myself known as a face from the sailing club and diplomatic parties, were on their way to a new posting and she remarked that it was to the West Indies this time, where, of course, the D——s were now; it would be good to have someone they already knew, when they got there, and the D——s had always been such fun, the island hadn't been the same since they left, had it? She would give them my best wishes, they would be glad to have news of their friends.

No letter. I did not expect one; I thought of him passionately as someone just as I was, ejected from the mould of myself, unrecognizable even to myself, spending nights in towns that while familiar (all the islands had the same palms, nightclubs, fruit-bats, the same creaking air conditioners and the long yawn of the sea) were not home. Being the distinguished man he was, the ambassador had been particularly friendly and amusing, once I had shown I was to be recognized in my new circumstances, but now that I was, theoretically, available, he did not try to see me again. The pilots were bored with their wives and pestered me. I slept in Curepipe one night with a Canadian businessman who felt it was fated because twice, three months apart, he had come to the islands and found me serving his whisky on the plane. I got what I wanted out of the encounter; a climax of sobbing and self-pity gave me back my yearning for my lover.

Long after, many months later, when I was home and my husband and I were having the house altered and the garden landscaped, there was a letter. *Are you mad? A mixture between a skivvy and a chorus-girl on one of those terrible old crates? What will happen to you?* How he must have struggled with himself, telling himself, as I did every day, there was no use to write. I would see my face in the mirror as if he were looking at it: only twenty-nine, thinner in the jaw since the drudgery and irregular hours of the airline, longer hair, now, and the haughty look that unhappiness and dissatisfaction give when you are still young. My husband had gone into the shipping business, on his own initiative; the island was about to run up the new flag as an independent state and he had ingratiated himself with the ruling coterie. I still couldn't speak a word of the language but I was one of the first white women to appear at official banquets wearing long, graceful, island dress. My husband became confidential financial adviser to the new black president; anyone from the foreign trade consulates who wanted privileges in the regime had to come to him, now.

There were riots down in the native town or the up-country districts but we really only were aware of them from the newspapers. The regime survived and my husband made a lot of money. His triumph in my return had opened a source of energy in him that nothing could check. Not that we had ever been poor; once you had a house in the bluff district, a swimming pool, and some sort of craft in the yacht club harbour, there wasn't much else money could add to life on the island. Anybody could have the sea, sun, the flowers for the picking and the oysters off the rocks. He wanted to send as Christmas cards pictures of the children taken with his super cameras but I flew out against it and he liked confidently to give in to my whims. He had to travel often to Europe and enjoyed taking me with him. I did a lot of shopping for myself; his greatest pleasure was to buy presents for the children, in particular pretty dresses for the girl. In those days my lady ran about the beach like a little bedraggled princess, wearing hand-tucked Liberty lawn as a bathing wrap—a wild and spoilt child. We used to have to visit my husband's mother who had retired to a hill village in the South of France and on one of these visits

I drove into Nice to shop. Sitting in a café open to and noisy as the street I found I had lost the car key; and it was there, in the telephone booth that smelled (I can still conjure it up at will) of sweaty feet and sour wine, while I was waiting distastefully for my call to the village, that I saw out of the scribblings on the dirty wall, a name.

Arno   Arno   Arno Arkanius

Someome had stood waiting for a connection in that telephone booth in that café and written, again and again, as you might pick up a stick and write on the sand where no one will read it, that name. There were many others jotted down, with numbers that belonged along with them: Pierre, Jan, Delphine, Marc, Maria, Horst, Robert. I read them all carefully. They were names common to thousands of men and women, but this name, this combination of first and surname—could it come about to signify another identity? I knew, as if my own hand had held that dark-leaded pencil (it was not a ball-point; a ball-point would never have written so clearly on that greasy wall), that this was he, this statement was about him and no other. Impossible to say who had made it, or when; only why. The telephone ring leapt counter to the dulled noise from without pressing upon the glass door and I spoke what I had to say, not taking my eyes off the wall. Arno Arno   Arno Arkanius. I hung up. I collected from the dirty floor my bag and parcels and went to the bar to pay for the call. So I had forgotten; somebody else wept and indulged erotic fantasies, somebody else pronounced the name as a devout Jew might secretly speak the forbidden name of Jehovah. While this had been happening I had forgotten, the baby with the big mouth had become my husband's child—it was true, I was deceived and not he, about her identity—because I had forgotten, for days, months on end. I had thought I was permanently unhappy but how could that be?—I had forgotten. There must be many children such as she, happy to be who they are, whose real identity could be resuscitated only if their mother's youth could be brought back to life again.

THE TERMITARY

When you live in a small town far from the world you read about in municipal library books, the advent of repair men in the house is a festival. Daily life is gaily broken open, improvisation takes over. The living-room masquerades as a bedroom while the smell of paint in the bedroom makes it uninhabitable. The secret backs of confident objects (matchwood draped with cobwebs thickened by dust) are given away when furniture is piled to the centre of the room. Meals are picnics at which table manners are suspended because the first principle of deportment drummed into children by their mother—sitting down at table—is missing: there is nowhere to sit. People are excused eccentricities of dress because no one can find anything in its place.

A doctor is also a kind of repair man. When he is expected the sheets are changed and the dog chased off the patient's bed. If a child is sick, she doesn't have to go to school, she is on holiday, with presents into the bargain—a whole roll of comics tied with newsagent's string, and crayons or card games. The mother is alone in the house, except for the patient out of earshot in the sickroom; the other children are at school. Her husband is away at work. She takes off her apron, combs her hair and puts on a bit of lipstick to make herself decent for the doctor, setting ready a tea-tray for two in the quiet privacy of the deserted living-room as for a secret morning visit from the lover she does not have. After she and the doctor, who smells intoxicating, coldly sweet because he has just come from the operating theatre, have stood together looking down at the patient and making jolly remarks, he is glad to accept a cup of tea in his busy morning round and their voices are a murmur and an occasional rise of laughter from behind the closed living-room door.

Plumber, painter, doctor; with their arrival something has happened where nothing ever happens; at home: a house with a bungalow face made of two bow-window eyes on either side of a front-door mouth, in a street in a gold-mining town of twenty-five thousand people in South Africa in the 1930s.

Once the upright Steinway piano stood alone on the few remaining boards of a room from which the floor had been ripped. I burst in to look at the time on the chiming clock that should have been standing on the mantelpiece and instead flew through the air and found myself jolted down into a subterranean smell of an earth I'd never smelt before, the earth buried by our house. I was nine years old and the drop broke no bones; the shock excited me, the thought of that hollow, earth-breaking dark always beneath our Axminster thrilled me; the importance I gained in my mother's accounts of how I might so easily have injured myself added to the sense of occasion usual in the family when there were workmen in.

This time it was not the painters, Mr Strydom and his boys, over whom my mother raised a quarrel every few years. *I'm not like any other woman. I haven't got a husband like other women's. The state this house is in. You'd see the place fall to pieces before you'd lift a finger. Too mean to pay for a lick of paint, and then when you do you expect it to last ten years. I haven't got a home like other women.* Workmen were treated as the house-guests we never had; my mother's friends were neighbours, my father had none, and she wouldn't give house-room to a spare bed, anyway, because she didn't want his relatives coming. Mr Strydom was served sweet strong tea to his taste many times a day, while my mother stood by to chat and I followed his skills with the brush, particularly fascinated when he was doing something he called, in his Afrikaner's English, 'pulling the line'. This was the free-hand deftness with which he could make a narrow black stripe dividing the lower half of our passage, painted dark against dirty fingerprints, from the cream upper half. *Yust a sec while I first pull the line, ay.*

Then he would drain his cup so completely that the tea leaves swirled up and stuck to the sides. This workmanlike thirst, for me, was a foreign custom, sign of the difference between being Afrikaans and English, as we were, just as I accepted that it must be in accordance with *their* custom that the black 'boys' drank their tea from jam tins in the yard. But Mr Strydom, like the doctor, like deaf dapper Mr Waite the electrician, who had drinking bouts because he had been through something called

Ypres, and Mr Hartman who sang to himself in a sad soprano while he tuned the Steinway upright my mother had brought from her own mother's house, was a recurrent event. The state the house was in, this time, was one without precedent; the men who were in were not repair men. They had been sent for to exterminate what we called white ants—termites who were eating our house away under our feet. A million jaws were devouring steadily night and day the timber that supported our unchanging routines: one day (if my mother hadn't done something about it you may be sure no one else would) that heavy Steinway in its real rosewood case would have crashed through the floor-boards.

For years my mother had efficiently kicked apart the finely-granulated earth, forming cones perfect as the shape taken by sand that has trickled through an egg-timer, that was piled in our garden by ordinary black ants. My father never did a hand's turn; she herself poured a tar-smelling disinfectant down the ant-holes and emptied into them kettles of boiling water that made the ground break out in a sweat of gleaming, struggling, pin-head creatures in paroxysm. Yet (it was another event) on certain summer evenings after rain we would rush out into the garden to be in the tropical snowfall of millions of transparent wings from what we called flying ants, who appeared from nowhere. We watched while frogs bold with greed hopped onto the verandah to fill their pouched throats with these apparently harmless insects, and our cat ate steadily but with more self-control, spitting out with a shake of her whiskers any fragment of wing she might have taken up by mistake. We did not know that when these creatures shed their four delicate dragon-fly wings (some seemed to struggle like people getting out of coats) and became drab terrestrials, and some idiotically lifted their hindquarters in the air as if they were reacting to injury, they were enacting a nuptial ceremony that, one summer night or another, had ended in one out of these millions being fertilized and making her way under our house to become queen of a whole colony generated and given birth to by herself. Somewhere under our house she was in an endless parturition that would go on until she was found and killed.

The men had been sent for to search out the queen. No evil-smelling poisons, no opening-up of the tunnels more skilfully constructed than the London Underground, the Paris Metro or the New York subway I'd read about, no fumigation such as might do for cockroaches or moles or wood-borer beetles, could eradicate termites. No matter how many thousands were killed by my mother, as, in the course of the excavations that tore up the floor-boards of her house, the brittle passages made of grains of earth cemented by a secretion carried in the termites' own bodies were broken, and the inhabitants poured out in a pus of white moving droplets with yellow heads—no matter how many she cast into death agony with her Flit spray, the termitary would at once be repopulated so long as the queen remained, alive, hidden in that inner chamber where her subjects who were also her progeny had walled her in and guarded and tended her.

The three exterminators were one white and two black. All had the red earth of underground clinging to their clothes and skin and hair; their eyes were bloodshot; the nails of their hands, black or white, were outlined in red, their ears rimmed. The long hairs in the nostrils of the white man were coated with red as a bee's legs are yellow with pollen. These men themselves appeared to have been dug up, raw from that clinging earth entombed beneath buildings. Bloodied by their life-long medieval quest, they were ready to take it up once more: the search for a queen. They were said to be very good; my mother was sceptical as she was about the powers of water-diviners with bent twigs or people who got the dead to spell out messages by moving a glass to letters of the alphabet. But what else could she do? My father left it all to her, she had the responsibility.

She didn't like the look of these men. They were so filthy with earth; hands like exposed roots reaching for the tea she brought. She served even the white man with a tin mug.

It was she who insisted they leave a few boards intact under the piano; she knew better than to trust them to move it without damage to the rosewood case. They didn't speak while children watched them at work. The only sound was the pick stopped by the density of the earth under our living-room, and the gasp of the black man who wielded the pick, pulling it free and hurling it back into the earth again. Held off by silence, we children would not go away. We stolidly spent all our free time in witness. Yet in spite of our vigilance, when it happened, when they found her, at last—the queen—we were not there.

My mother was mixing a cake and we had been attracted away to her by that substance of her alchemy that was not the beaten eggs and butter and sugar that went into it; even the lightest stroke of a quick forefinger into the bowl conveyed a coating of fragrant creamy sweetness to the mouth which already had foreknowledge of its utter satisfaction through the scent of vanilla that came not only from the bowl, but from her clothes, her hair, her very skin. Suddenly my mother's dog lifted his twitching lip back over his long teeth and began to bounce towards and back away from the screen door as he did when any stranger approached her. We looked up; the three men had come to the back steps. The white gestured his ochre hand brusquely at one of the blacks, who tramped forward with a child's cardboard shoe-box offered. The lid was on and there were rough air-holes punched in it here and there, just as in the boxes where we had kept silk worms until my mother thought they smelled too musty and threw them away. The white man gestured again; he and my mother for a moment held their hands the same way, his covered with earth, hers with flour. The black man took off the lid.

And there she was, the queen. The smallest child swallowed as if about to retch and ran away to the far side of the kitchen. The rest of us crowded nearer, but my mother made us make way, she wasn't going to be fobbed off with anything but complete satisfaction for her husband's money. We all gazed at an obese, helpless white creature, five inches long, with the tiny, shiny-visored head of an ant at one end. The body was a sort of dropsical sac attached to this head; it had no legs that could be seen, neither could it propel itself by peristaltic action, like a slug or worm. The queen. The queen whose domain, we had seen for ourselves in the galleries and passages that had been uncovered beneath our house, was as big as ours.

The white man spoke. 'That's 'er, missus.'

'You're sure you've got the queen?'

'We got it. That's it.' He gave a professional snigger at ignorance.

Was she alive? —But again the silence of the red-eyed, red-earthed men kept us back; they wouldn't let us daringly put out a finger to touch that body that seemed blown up in sections, like certain party balloons, and that had at once the suggestion of tactile attraction and repugnance—if a finger were to be stroked testingly along that perhaps faintly downy body, sweet creamy stuff might be expected to ooze from it. And in fact, when I found a book in the library called *The Soul of the White Ant*, by Eugène Marais, an Afrikaner like the white man who had found the queen's secret chamber, I read that the children-subjects at certain times draw nourishment from a queen's great body by stroking it so that she exudes her own rich maternal elixir.

'Ughh. Why's she so fat?' The smallest child had come close enough to force himself to look again.

'S'es full of ecks,' the white man said. 'They lays about a million ecks a day.'

'Is it dead?'

But the man only laughed, now that his job was done, and like the showman's helper at the conclusion of an act, the black man knew to clap the lid back on the shoe-box. There was no way for us to tell; the queen cannot move, she is blind; whether she is underground, the tyrannical prisoner of her subjects who would not have been born and cannot live without her, or whether she is captured and borne away in a shoe-box, she is helpless to evade the consequences of her power.

My mother paid the men out of her housekeeping allowance (but she would have to speak to our father about that) and they nailed back the living-room floor-boards and went away, taking the cardboard box with them. My mother had heard that the whole thing was a hoax; these men went from house to house, made the terrible mess they'd left hers in, and produced the same queen time and again, carrying it around with them.

Yet the termites left our house. We never had to have those particular workmen in again. The Axminster carpet was laid once more, the furniture put back in its place, and I had to do the daily half-hour practice on the Steinway that I had been freed of for a week. I read in the book from the library that when the queen dies or is taken away all the termites leave their posts and desert the termitary; some find their way to other communities, thousands die. The termitary with its fungus-gardens for food, its tunnels for conveying water from as much as forty feet underground, its elaborate defence and communications system, is abandoned.

We lived on, above the ruin. The children grew up and left the town; coming back from the war after 1946 and later from visits to Europe and America and the Far East, it bored them to hear the same old stories, to be asked: 'D'you remember Mr Hartman who used to come in to tune the piano? He was asking after you the other day—poor thing, he's crippled with arthritis.' 'D'you remember old Strydom, "pulling the line"...how you kids used to laugh, I was quite ashamed...' 'D'you remember the time the white ant men were in, and you nearly broke your leg?' Were these events the sum of my mother's life? Why should I remember? I, who—shuddering to look back at those five rooms behind the bow-window eyes and the front-door mouth—have oceans, continents, snowed-in capitals, islands where turtles swim, cathedrals, theatres, palace gardens where people kiss and tramps drink wine—all these to remember. My father grew senile and she put him in a home for his last years. She stayed on, although she said she didn't want to; the house was a burden to her, she had carried the whole responsibility for him, for all of us, all her life. Now she is dead and although I suppose someone else lives in her house, the secret passages, the inner chamber in which she was our queen and our prisoner are sealed up, empty.

THE NEED FOR SOMETHING SWEET

It seems like a long life. Once I even tried to cure a woman who was an alcoholic. That was when I was in the Civil Service, I remember how I met her, she was sitting with her legs crossed on the broken chair opposite my counter at the GPO when I came from lunch. She wore bottle-green stockings and her shins shone through. There were several other people waiting to make long-distance telephone calls. That was my job at the time: I had two or three phones in front of me, a book to enter codes, numbers and names, a cash-box, and I spent my days dialling International and directing people to the booths where they could take calls. Monotonous on my side of the counter; plenty of excitement and worry on the other side. Nobody ever came in there calm. They shouted so loudly across the undersea cables, I could hear what was being said through the glass of the booths—not that I understood a word, most of them were foreigners, immigrants phoning home to Italy, Spain, France, Greece, Portugal and Germany.

Anita Gonzalez, I remember you.

Hers was person-to-person, reverse charges, to her husband in a small Spanish town. At least she used his name, although she told me later they were not married, he had left the country and she was trying to trace him by telephoning his family and letting them think he had married overseas—he had come to South Africa as a hotel manager. If they knew him as she did they would be just as likely to believe her as him. But the call was not successful; the manual exchange at that village had no one who could speak English, there was some muddle—I said perhaps she ought to try again in the morning. Next day the call went through all right, but the party at the other end wouldn't accept charges. I know that I used the usual formula—'Are you prepared to pay yourself, then?' And she said: 'Forget it.' You get accustomed to people being, you know, emotional, in a job like that. I used to see them laughing and crying as they came out of those booths, and some stood over me and wouldn't believe it when calls rang and rang in empty rooms across the world, or the wrong voice answered.

We were alone in that office that morning. I offered a cup of coffee from my ten o'clock thermos. She was a good-looker marked by signs I was too green to read. She was black-haired and high-coloured on the cheekbones with lines like cuts in the flesh curved from the inside corner of each eye to just below the point of the cheekbone. She said one thing, though (I didn't take any notice at the time): 'You don't realize it will all happen to you.' Then she laughed and joked with me about the people I had to deal with in my job. I enjoyed telling my stories. Her lips twitched and curled in sympathy, mimicking after me. When she left I said I was sorry she hadn't been able to take her call, and asked whether she would be back to try once more? (I guessed that she didn't have the money and might raise it.) She said: 'Never.' I saw then that she was much older than I was; I suddenly wanted to pay for the call myself: all at once I was one of those others, on the other side of the counter, who didn't know what to say, helpless. I couldn't go after the sound of the woman's heels down the post office corridor. I couldn't call her back even if I bellowed the way they did, down the phone. Right away there was something that only ever happened to me with that woman; not just the usual swelling but an actual pulse beating down there, like you can find in your wrist or the way you can feel your heart in your chest. There was the name I'd written in my register (I didn't know then it wasn't her real name); but we didn't ask for people's addresses—I had no way of finding out where the sound of those heels was taking her.

And yet I was not really surprised when I found myself in a department store lift with her three days later. The attendant told someone smoking was not allowed. As the person in question twisted her cigarette into the tray of sand provided, that person became her. My shift at the post office was over for the day, the store was closing; I stuck close by her in the crowd pushing through the main exit and I asked if she was coming from work. 'I've just got up,' she said, telling me a secret. I don't know what she had come out to buy; she must have been too late because she had no packet or parcel. I said, 'Can I walk with you a bit?' I was too scared to ask to take her for a cup of tea somewhere but I had come to her heels, a puppy-dog who wouldn't be shaken off now, whatever happened. 'I'm not all that keen on fresh air,' she said. She smiled as if she thought she ought to get rid of me but couldn't bring herself to.

We went into the lounge bar in the old Langham Hotel and that was the beginning of it. I didn't get back to my boarding-house for dinner, I didn't get back home that night at all. We sat there until about ten o'clock, me spinning out three bottles of beer and she solidly drinking brandy and Coke, and then, although she couldn't walk straight, she argued against my taking her home and refused to tell me the address. This drunk woman, like a schoolmistress, telling me what's good for me. Then the barman gave me her address. I suppose he'd had to put her into a taxi, before. I carried her into the building and felt her arms round my neck as something to hang on to, I could've been anyone. I found her key in the pocket of her coat and entered the place where she lived: an immigrant's bachelor flat that'd been lived in by a lot of different people who'd come and gone—if I'd been older, I'd have been able to realize that from the empty picture-shapes on the walls, the foreign names scribbled round a calendar, the squeaking of the broken divan springs as I laid her down, just as I'd have been able to tell from her face what she was. The bed had another one that pulled out from underneath it and I slept there in my clothes because I was afraid something might happen to her—I don't know what, I'd never seen a woman motherless-drunk before. I thought she might die; or rather that I might lose her again, at once, she might wake up and go away. I wrote down the address of the flat I was in and put it in my 21st-birthday-present wallet in a special extra pocket that had been empty until then, I'd wondered what it was for, as a matter of fact. Now it held the address and I slept knowing that's what was pressing against my ribs.

In the morning she felt terrible. She said the bones of her feet ached and I held her feet to warm in my hands, a little bony bump on each instep, long weakly-moving second toes, the damp, stretched nylons holding the shape of each foot and smelling a little sour, but of her, it was part of her.

I was late for work. Man, I was happy. I'd said to her, you stay in bed. I know I rushed back to her flat in my lunch-hour with a can of soup, beef broth, and a new can-opener from the shop where we'd met. We laughed at the night before, she said she couldn't think what had happened—'You know? Sometimes just two drinks and you feel it. On an empty stomach, or if you've been worried or upset or something. You know?' And I truly didn't know any more what I knew, that she had drunk half a bottle of brandy.

She was not a slut, in spite of her drinking—at least not at the stage I knew her. She had got up and bathed and put scent on herself and made her bed properly; she had on one of those Spanish shawls with shiny embroidery and fringe over her nightdress, and you could see now that she was certainly not young, there were soft creases in her neck and her ribs weren't showing like a young girl's but her breasts and her arms were marvellous, still plumped up, moving about; so lively, as she told me where I'd find this and that in the kitchenette. That other throbbing started the moment I came into a room where she was; it was always like that. When I got into the bed and felt against me what I'd been looking at (seemed to me) since the time she sat there in front of me at the post office, the two hearts in my body beat with such weight and slowness I thought I would stop breathing. Honest to God.

She must have let me fuck her that first time to make up for letting me see her drunk. To take me in her arms not just as something to hang on to. I think she felt sorry for me. I don't know what she felt; people who drink tell so many lies. They have to, so as to be let go on drinking; so as to cheat themselves when they've decided to keep off the drink. She told me all sorts of stories about her life; they ended abruptly and usually didn't fit with others she'd told before. For instance she talked about her mother and then said how she'd never known a mother, was brought up by an aunt who hated her. I hadn't heard many hard-luck stories in my life, then. I didn't recognize that one. The aunt came on the scene in her stories when it had happened again several times—I'd found her drunk—she couldn't pretend any longer that it was something unusual for her. She'd been unhappy as a kid, she'd made a stupid marriage at sixteen to get away from home: et cetera; of course. But it was all new to me.

And yet some of the things she told couldn't have been made up—who would have thought of the business of the cold bath, for instance? When she disappeared for two days and I knew she was drunk somewhere and I was out of my mind, afterwards we lay in her bed together like two weak people recovering from an accident and I had my eyes closed and a thick band of her hair to breathe through, laid across my face—that was when she told about the cold bath. She was sixteen, an older man took a fancy to her (she never said so, but she must have been a beauty) and thought it a joke to make her tipsy at a party. At her home her aunt opened the front door and saw her giggling there, held up by the man. (That was the first time: I suppose that was what she meant to tell me.) 'I just wanted my aunt to smile at me, that's all. Just to give me a smile. She used to keep those sucking sweets, Glacier Mints—look like little glass bricks, you know?—to give us if we'd been specially good, and I waited for her to smile like the way I used to wait to see, while I was little, whether I'd get a sweet or not, I'd watch her about the house, every movement, needing that sweet. She had the man and my uncle carry me to the bathroom and she ran the bath full to the top with cold water, and she took off my clothes in front of them and made them put me in. I was so cold, my God it was cold. She held me down. Then I was sick and she wouldn't help me. So cold, so cold, the water. I was such a silly kid, I'd really waited for that smile when she came to the door. I didn't *know* she hated me.'

'Why'd she hate you?'

The rosy-pink flesh between her eyes and those cuts across the cheekbones was puffy because of the way she had spent the past few days, and her beautiful eyes had red veins against the blue, under the plucked shape of shining black eyebrows and eyelashes that made me think of the special soft brush with flowers painted on the back that was used to clear away crumbs from the table in our house on the farm. But she said, like a young girl—and I was crazy about her when she was so proud and catty and natural, you'd think there couldn't be anything wrong with her: 'Jealous. Because of my hair. You could see her scalp through hers.' That black hair was something to envy, all right. The high colouring was her own (real Irish colouring, from her grandfather) but I suppose the hair must have had dye on it when I knew her.

Another time she told the story of the cold bath as something she had done to her daughter—the daughter she'd lost touch with, didn't know where she lived now, child of that 'lousy marriage' she didn't talk of much. She blamed herself for behaving like a fool, losing her head over the poor kid. And by now I understood that she was saying that it happened because she was a drinker herself and had to punish drinkers. 'All the kid needed was someone to say something nice. So she wouldn't be scared.'

I was also beginning to understand that drinking divides people up inside themselves—peculiar, it is—so that they become several different people, all different stages of life, in the one body. All these different girls and women in that woman put the blame on each other for what she was. What was done to her and what she had done were the same, to her.

Of course I got the idea I could cure her. The mad idea of taking her to our farm, to start with. My elder brother and his wife, who were running the place then because my father was already bedridden, were teetotallers, signed the pledge. There wasn't a drop in the house. I didn't tell her my annual leave wasn't due and I'd wangled three weeks, unpaid, on grounds that my father was dying and there was no one to look after the farm. I wanted to get her away, out of town, all to myself, as soon as possible. I don't know how I managed to make the family swallow the story: you, Anita Gonzalez, were the widow of my best friend, a chap who worked with me at the post office in Johannesburg, and you were recovering from an illness brought on by the shock of his death.

I told them they must not mention her husband, ever. I don't remember what I told her. Any strangeness about her they put down to nerves; that I should spend so much of my holiday walking around the farm with her I hoped they would put down to a death-bed promise to my friend. Once I lived in town I thought the country people I came from would believe that kind of thing.

The first few days were heaven—for me. She was put in the rondavel down under the syringas because she needed peace and quiet away from my brother's children—and because I intended to slip out of the house and sleep with her every night. I don't know what she thought. I don't know why she came; the money the Spanish hotel manager had left her was finished, I suppose, perhaps she thought she really was giving up drinking; one of the people inside her always believed she was making a fresh start.

My brother was running chickens, on the side—day-old chicks to stock the battery-raised table market—and she helped me feed them, tapping the old oil-drums so that the bran I was tipping in at the top came through the holes round the bottom at the right rate to fill the troughs. She'd lived in towns and was surprised at the sense animals and birds have; everything they did was a wonder to her. Walking round the mealie fields we'd find V-shaped spoor and diggings made by the same buck; she'd call me to look how the hole was a V, too, because the hoof can only scrape its own shape. Aardvark burrows appeared to her to have been made by something with fingers and hands—they made her shudder. I wished I could have shown her the nice harmless old creature, but you'll never see one about during the day. I fished a bit for black bass in the dam but it was only to have her there, getting a suntan, beside me, us hidden by the mound of the dam wall. The glossy starlings on the telephone wires were just the colour of her hair in the sun. She didn't know how to ride and was afraid of horses but like all women she wanted to touch the new-born calves. She tried to make a pet of one of the half-wild yard-kittens and it scratched her neck right across from under the ear to the swelling of her breast; when my sister-in-law was putting mercurochrome on the scratch while I stood by I saw from the look on her face that they knew the little brother was sleeping with this woman and didn't like it.

What I never understood was how much she must have been suffering on that farm. I was such a kid. I suppose I must have known that the love-making every night, when I came across late to her room, for some reason, now, couldn't give her any pleasure, it wasn't any good to her. It would have been hard to believe that anything that drove me so wild, that I waited for, throbbing, all day, watching her, could fail. I couldn't help being happy. One night when she cried and cried, saying 'I can't, I can't,' I thought she meant the love-making and I felt a terrible disappointment, a foreboding at being turned away to the kind of life, without a woman, I used to have before. I didn't know what to do. If only I could have told someone—my brother. But I didn't dare, I'd lose her. The loneliness, in a place like Johannesburg, when a youngster hasn't got a lot of money to throw around. If only someone would have said to me: it's all right.

And then she would roam around the farm all day, disappear and not come back for meals, and I'd have to go asking the farm natives, even the piccanins, if they'd seen her. She didn't know any Afrikaans so she couldn't talk to them, but once or twice I found her playing with these black kids, they were laughing at her —she asked me to let them ride on the tractor I'd taken to come after her. Specially in the late afternoon, she'd go off and walk for miles, me beside her, but more as if I were following, because it seemed she couldn't talk to me. With our two shadows running along ahead, she seemed to know where we were going. She chewed grass-stalks and spat. Once she stopped dead at that bush full of yellow berries we call stinkblaar. I said, 'It's poison. We know about it as kids—just one and it's finished.' And then there was the thorn tree where the finches used to sleep. I'd been looking for her—she'd gone off while I was helping my brother put up a fence—and I ran into her at that tree. The flock flew between us and dropped like a table-cloth over the tree—it's a lovely sight, I was glad she'd got the chance to see it. As we approached, the birds were disturbed and blew themselves in gusts from one branch to another. There were thousands, no bigger than your thumb, pale blue and fawn, twittering, the volume turned up ringing in your ears. She was saying something and I actually couldn't even hear what. Then the whole flying carpet took off. I heard her say—and she would come to me often, again, after that, about sunset, and say it: 'I want to drink—make love to me.'

What could I do. There, in the field? With the herd-boy or some piccanin coming along any time; my brother, perhaps, I couldn't take her to the rondavel during the day. She knew that. My brother's kids playing in the garden, running in and out.

We did it once or twice. Clothes opened just enough to get at each other. Afterwards she went to the rondavel and slept, didn't come to supper. My sister-in-law shrugged and took away the plate, knife and fork laid for her.

They found out about her because she drank the children's cough medicine. They said a bottle of methylated spirits, too, but I don't believe that, I think the kitchen boy put the blame on her. They told me she was much older than I said, she was at least fifteen years older than I was, and I was nothing but a kid, throwing my life away. They were right. I howled like a baby in front of them. I was afraid of only one thing—they would take her. I would never be inside her again, the sweet pleasure would never be there however long I waited. I couldn't tell them that. They got the dominee to see me after church; I was rude to him. I said if they sent her away they wouldn't ever see me again. But they talked to her, not about the drink but about the difference in ages, and she went. They were right. She said, 'Stay for the rest of your leave. Don't make a fuss. I'll be at the flat.' They brought neighbours' daughters to the farm and they made me go to dances. I didn't look at any girl.

But they were right.

Anita Gonzalez.

She was right: when she said in the post office that time, you don't realize it will all happen to you. Thirty-one years ago. I don't often remember her; as I've had to tell my own sons, there's more to life than chasing women. I've had a hard struggle to make my way and the main thing is to have a wife who will work with you, keep a decent home like the one they've been lucky enough to have. Twice I've lost everything and had to start again; the building industry carries big risks but I've come a long, long way from the junior salary scale at the GPO. I went into partnership with someone who fleeced me but I've paid out people like him ten times over, with interest, believe me. You learn to look after yourself and not worry about what people call you. You start out with nothing and everything's going to happen to you. Your gums give trouble, they tell you you must cut down on fats and drink, no salt because of blood pressure. No matter how many women you've had, the girls on the beach don't even see you, any more. That's natural. Between husband and wife, it's the things you've got in common—the children and grandchildren, the investments and property—that are the bond in the end. The rest dies down. It's natural. When I went back to Johannesburg eventually, that woman was always expecting me to come to the flat. If I didn't turn up she'd phone the post office or come to look for me. I'd get a message: Your sister or mother or whoever-she-is was here. It was embarrassing for a youngster. I was making friends my own age. I had to give her money and I wasn't exactly flush, myself. Once I'd left the post office, she didn't know where to find me. Poor creature. I see those sherry-gang women in the parks, I realize she could be one of them. Good looks don't last, even if a woman leads a decent life. Who would believe a clean youngster could get mixed up with a woman who could end up like that. Anita Gonzalez—that's the name I wrote in the register, all those years ago, but God knows what her real name was, I've long forgotten.

I remembered her only this evening when I walked out of the hotel just before dinner. I'd had a few words with the wife; nothing much, the usual thing between people who've been married a long time. I usually come alone on business trips and maybe it's better that way. My wife is one of those people who don't answer back but put you in the wrong by giving in. If I strike an employee who's like that, I get rid of him immediately. I came out of the hotel to be alone for a bit and get some exercise and I walked about a mile along the sea-front. My wife's put on a lot of weight, like her mother before her, those women won't stir without a car. I noticed the old seal enclosure they've always had here and I walked down the steps from the promenade to see if the seals are still alive. It's humid on this coast; at once I could smell them. But it's a natural stink, and there was the salt of the sea as well. I was alone there as you are in a place that would be full of people gaping and teasing the poor beasts during the day—potato-crisp packets and orange peel left all over the cement. The bull seal was out of the water and lying quite still on his back with his jaws open the way they wait to be fed a fish, or anything they've learned to expect

—people throwing peanuts and sweets at them. The sea slopped gently over into the enclosure; it was the only sound. The cows were gliding silently underwater before him, circling and looping without breaking the light running over the surface. His shadow was long on-the concrete. So was mine. The seals did not know anyone was there. He gave a grunt that didn't close his gaping snout, taking in the air of the open sea beyond. The cows in the water slid their heads out without a ripple and downed again, weaving in and out past each other's shapes. The coming night buried them in dark water; soon I could hardly make out they were there. And the seal lay, alone, mouth open—hungry, perhaps?—I didn't understand.

You were right, it happens, it's always all to come. You can't sit there the rest of the night. You've got to get up, walk back to the hotel. You're expected. And you'll be there in fifteen minutes at the most, no matter how you take your time.

ORAL HISTORY

There's always been one house like a white man's house in the village of Dilolo. Built of brick with a roof that bounced signals from the sun. You could see it through the mopane trees as you did the flash of paraffin tins the women carried on their heads, bringing water from the river. The rest of the village was built of river mud, grey, shaped by the hollows of hands, with reed thatch and poles of mopane from which the leaves had been ripped like fish-scales.

It was the chief's house. Some chiefs have a car as well but this was not an important chief, the clan is too small for that, and he had the usual stipend from the government. If they had given him a car he would have had no use for it. There is no road: the army patrol Land Rovers come upon the people's cattle, startled as buck, in the mopane scrub. The village has been there a long time. The chief's grandfather was the clan's grandfathers' chief, and his name is the same as that of the chief who waved his warriors to down assegais and took the first bible from a Scottish Mission Board white man. *Seek and ye shall find*, the missionaries said.

The villagers in those parts don't look up, any more, when the sting-shaped army planes fly over twice a day. Only fish-eagles are disturbed, take off, screaming, keen swerving heads lifting into their invaded domain of sky. The men who have been away to work on the mines can read, but there are no newspapers. The people hear over the radio the government's count of how many army trucks have been blown up, how many white soldiers are going to be buried with *full military honours*—something that is apparently white people's way with their dead.

The chief had a radio, and he could read. He read to the headmen the letter from the government saying that anyone hiding or giving food and water to those who were fighting against the government's army would be put in prison. He read another letter from the government saying that to protect the village from these

134

men who went over the border and came back with guns to kill people and burn huts, anybody who walked in the bush after dark would be shot. Some of the young men who, going courting or drinking to the next village, might have been in danger, were no longer at home in their fathers' care, anyway. The young go away: once it was to the mines, now—the radio said—it was over the border to learn how to fight. Sons walked out of the clearing of mud huts; past the chief's house; past the children playing with the models of police patrol Land Rovers made out of twisted wire. The children called out, Where are you going? The young men didn't answer and they hadn't come back.

There was a church of mopane and mud with a mopane flagpole to fly a white flag when somebody died; the funeral service was more or less the same protestant one the missionaries brought from Scotland and it was combined with older rituals to entrust the newly-dead to the ancestors. Ululating women with whitened faces sent them on their way to the missionaries' last judgment. The children were baptized with names chosen by portent in consultation between the mother and an old man who read immutable fate in the fall of small bones cast like dice from a horn cup. On all occasions and most Saturday nights there was a beer-drink, which the chief attended. An upright chair from his house was brought out for him although everyone else squatted comfortably on the sand, and he was offered the first taste from an old decorated gourd dipper (other people drank from baked-bean or pilchard tins)—it is the way of people of the village.

It is also the way of the tribe to which the clan belongs and the subcontinent to which the tribe belongs, from Matadi in the west to Mombasa in the east, from Entebbe in the north to Empangeni in the south, that everyone is welcome at a beer-drink. No traveller or passer-by, poling down the river in his pirogue, leaving the snake-skin trail of his bicycle wheels through the sand, betraying his approach—if the dogs are sleeping by the cooking fires and the children have left their home-made highways—only by the brittle fragmentation of the dead leaves as he comes unseen through miles of mopane, is a presence to be questioned. Everyone for a long way round on both sides of the border near Dilolo has a black skin, speaks the same language and shares the custom of hospitality. Before the government started to shoot people at night to stop more young men leaving when no one was awake to ask, 'Where are you going?' people thought nothing of walking ten miles from one village to another for a beer-drink.

But unfamiliar faces have become unusual. If the firelight caught such a face, it backed into darkness. No one remarked the face. Not even the smallest child who never took its eyes off it, crouching down among the knees of men with soft, little boy's lips held in wonderingly over teeth as if an invisible grown-up hand were clamped there. The young girls giggled and flirted from the background, as usual. The older men didn't ask for news of relatives or friends outside the village. The chief seemed not to see one face or faces in distinction from any other. His eyes came to rest instead on some of the older men. He gazed and they felt it.

Coming out of the back door of his brick house with its polished concrete steps, early in the morning, he hailed one of them. The man was passing with his hobbling cows and steadily bleating goats; stopped, with the turn of one who will continue on his way in a moment almost without breaking step. But the summons was for him. The chief wore a frayed collarless shirt and old trousers, like the man, but he was never barefoot. In the hand with a big steel watch on the wrist, he carried his thick-framed spectacles, and drew down his nose between the fingers of the other hand; he had the authoritative body of a man who still has his sexual powers but his eyes flickered against the light of the sun and secreted flecks of matter like cold cream at the corners. After the greetings usual between a chief and one of his headmen together with whom, from the retreat in the mopane forest where they lay together in the same age-group recovering from circumcision, he had long ago emerged a man, the chief said, 'When is your son coming back?'

'I have no news.'

'Did he sign for the mines?'

'No.'

'He's gone to the tobacco farms?'

'He didn't tell us.'

'Gone away to find work and doesn't tell his mother? What sort of child is that? Didn't you teach him?'

The goats were tongue-ing three hunchback bushes that were all that was left of a hedge round the chief's house. The man took out a round tin dented with child's tooth-marks and taking care not to spill any snuff, dosed himself. He gestured at the beasts, for permission: 'They're eating up your house...' He made a move towards the necessity to drive them on.

'There is nothing left there to eat.' The chief ignored his hedge, planted by his oldest wife who had been to school at the mission up the river. He stood among the goats as if he would ask more questions. Then he turned and went back to his yard, dismissing himself. The other man watched. It seemed he might call after; but instead drove his animals with the familiar cries, this time unnecessarily loud and frequent.

Often an army patrol Land Rover came to the village. No one could predict when this would be because it was not possible to count the days in between and be sure that so many would elapse before it returned, as could be done in the case of a tax-collector or cattle-dipping officer. But it could be heard minutes away, crashing through the mopane like a frightened animal, and dust hung marking the direction from which it was coming. The children ran to tell. The women went from hut to hut. One of the chief's wives would enjoy the importance of bearing the news: 'The government is coming to see you.' He would be out of his house when the Land Rover stopped and a black soldier (murmuring towards the chief the required respectful greeting in their own language) jumped out and opened the door for the white soldier. The white soldier had learned the names of all the local chiefs. He gave greetings with white men's brusqueness: 'Everything all right?' And the chief repeated to him: 'Everything is all right.' 'No one been bothering you in this village?' 'No one is troubling us.' But the white soldier signalled to his black men and they went through every hut busy as wives when they are cleaning, turning over bedding, thrusting gun-butts into the pile of ash and rubbish where the chickens searched, even looking in, their eyes dazzled by darkness, to the hut where one of the old women who had gone crazy had to be kept most of the time. The white soldier stood beside the Land Rover waiting for them. He told the chief of things that were happening not far from the village; not far at all. The road that passed five kilometres away had been blown up. 'Someone plants land-mines in the road and as soon as we repair it they put them there again. Those people come from across the river and they pass this way. They wreck our vehicles and kill people.'

The heads gathered round weaved as if at the sight of bodies laid there horrifyingly before them.

'They will kill you, too—burn your huts, all of you—if you let them stay with you.'

A woman turned her face away: 'Aīe-aīe-aīe-aīe.'

His forefinger half-circled his audience. 'I'm telling you. You'll see what they do.'

The chief's latest wife, taken only the year before and of the age-group of his elder grandchildren, had not come out to listen to the white man. But she heard from others what he had said, and fiercely smoothing her legs with grease, demanded of the chief, 'Why does he want us to die, that white man!'

Her husband, who had just been a passionately shuddering lover, became at once one of the important old with whom she did not count and could not argue. 'You talk about things you don't know. Don't speak for the sake of making a noise.'

To punish him, she picked up the strong, young girl's baby she had borne him and went out of the room where she slept with him on the big bed that had come down the river by barge, before the army's machine guns were pointing at the other bank.

He appeared at his mother's hut. There, the middle-aged man on whom the villagers depended, to whom the government looked when it wanted taxes paid and culling orders carried out, became a son—the ageless category, no matter from which age-group to another he passed in the progression of her life and his. The old woman was at her toilet. The great weight of her body settled around her where she sat on a reed mat outside the door. He pushed a stool under himself. Set out was a small mirror with a pink plastic frame and stand, in which he caught sight of his face, screwed up. A large black comb; a little carved box inlaid with red lucky beans she had always had, he used to beg to be allowed to play with it fifty years ago. He waited, not so much out of respect as in the bond of indifference to all outside their mutual contact that reasserts itself when lions and their kin lie against one another.

She cocked a glance, swinging the empty loops of her stretched ear-lobes. He did not say what he had come for.

She had chosen a tiny bone spoon from the box and was poking with trembling care up each round hole of distended nostril. She cleaned the crust of dried snot and dust from her delicate instrument and flicked the dirt in the direction away from him.

She said: 'Do you know where your sons are?'

'Yes, I know where my sons are. You have seen three of them here today. Two are in school at the mission. The baby—he's with the mother.' A slight smile, to which the old woman did not respond. Her preferences among the sons had no connection with sexual pride.

'Good. You can be glad of all that. But don't ask other people about theirs.'

As often when people who share the same blood share the same thought, for a moment mother and son looked exactly alike, he old-womanish, she mannish.

'If the ones we know are missing, there are not always empty places,' he said.

She stirred consideringly in her bulk. Leaned back to regard him: 'It used to be that all children were our own children. All sons our sons. *Old-fashion*, these people here'—the hard English word rolled out of their language like a pebble, and came to rest where aimed, at his feet.

It was spring: the mopane leaves turn, drying up and dying, spattering the sand with blood and rust—a battlefield, it must have looked, from the patrol planes. In August there is no rain to come for two months yet. Nothing grows but the flies hatch. The heat rises daily and the nights hold it, without a stir, till morning. On these nights the radio voice carried so clearly it could be heard from the chief's house all through the village. Many were being captured in the bush and killed by the army—*seek and destroy* was what the white men said now—and many in the army were being set upon in the bush or blown up in their trucks and buried with full military honours. This was expected to continue until October because the men in the bush knew that it was their last chance before the rains came and chained their feet in mud.

On these hot nights when people cannot sleep anyway, beer-drinks last until very late. People drink more; the women know this, and brew more. There is a fire but no one sits close round it.

Without a moon the dark is thick with heat; when the moon is full the dark shimmers thinly in a hot mirage off the river. Black faces are blue, there are watermarks along noses and biceps. The chief sat on his chair and wore shoes and socks in spite of the heat; those drinking nearest him could smell the suffering of his feet. The planes of jaw and lips he noticed in moonlight molten over them, moonlight pouring moths broken from white cases on the mopane and mosquitoes rising from the river, pouring glory like the light in the religious pictures people got at the mission—he had seen those faces about lately in the audacity of day, as well. An ox had been killed and there was the scent of meat sizzling in the village (just look at the behaviour of the dogs, they knew) although there was no marriage or other festival that called for someone to slaughter one of his beasts. When the chief allowed himself, at least, to meet the eyes of a stranger, the whites that had been showing at an oblique angle disappeared and he took rather than saw the full gaze of the seeing eye: the pupils with their defiance, their belief, their claim, hold, on him. He let it happen only once. For the rest, he saw their arrogant lifted jaws to each other and warrior smiles to the girls, as they drank. The children were drawn to them, fighting one another silently for places close up. Towards midnight —his watch had its own glowing galaxy—he left his chair and did not come back from the shadows where men went to urinate.

Often at beer-drinks the chief would go home while others were still drinking.

He went to his brick house whose roof shone almost bright as day. He did not go to the room where his new wife and sixth son would be sleeping in the big bed, but simply took from the kitchen, where it was kept when not in use, a bicycle belonging to one of his hangers-on, relative or retainer. He wheeled it away from the huts in the clearing, his village and grandfather's village that disappeared so quickly behind him in the mopane, and began to ride through the sand. He was not afraid he would meet a patrol and be shot; alone at night in the sand forest, the forested desert he had known before and would know beyond his span of life, he didn't believe in the power of a roving band of government men to end that life. The going was heavy but he had mastered when young the art of riding on this, the only terrain he knew, and the ability came back. In an hour he arrived at the army post, called out who he was to the sentry with a machine gun, and had to wait, like a beggar rather than a chief, to be allowed to approach and be searched. There were black soldiers on duty but they woke the white man. It was the one who knew his name, his clan, his village, the way these modern white men were taught. He seemed to know at once why the chief had come; frowning in concentration to grasp details, his mouth was open in a smile and the point of his tongue curled touching at back teeth the way a man will verify facts one by one on his fingers. 'How many?'

'Six or ten or—but sometimes it's only, say, three or one...I don't know. One is here, he's gone; they come again.'

'They take food, they sleep, and off. Yes. They make the people give them what they want, that's it, eh? And you know who it is who hides them—who shows them where to sleep—of course you know.'

The chief sat on one of the chairs in that place, the army's place, and the white soldier was standing. 'Who is it—' the chief was having difficulty in saying what he wanted in English, he had the feeling it was not coming out as he had meant nor being understood as he had expected. 'I can't know who is it'—a hand moved restlessly, he held a breath and released it—'in the village there's many, plenty people. If it's this one or this one—' He stopped, shaking his head with a reminder to the white man of his authority, which the white soldier was quick to placate. 'Of course. Never mind. They frighten the people; the people can't say no. They kill people who say no, eh; cut their ears off, you know that? Tear away their lips. Don't you see the pictures in the papers?'

'We never saw it. I heard the government say on the radio.'

'They're still drinking... How long—an hour ago?'

The white soldier checked with a look the other men, whose stance had changed to that of bodies ready to break into movement: grab weapons, run, fling themselves at the Land Rovers guarded in the dark outside. He picked up the telephone receiver but blocked the mouth-piece as if it were someone about to make an objection. 'Chief, I'll be with you in a moment. —Take him to the duty room and make coffee. Just wait—' he leaned his full reach towards a drawer in a cabinet on the left of the desk and, scrabbling to get it open, took out a half-full bottle of brandy. Behind the chief's back he gestured the bottle towards the chief, and a black soldier jumped obediently to take it.

The chief went to a cousin's house in a village the other side of the army post later that night. He said he had been to a beer-drink and could not ride home because of the white men's curfew.

The white soldier had instructed that he should not be in his own village when the arrests were made so that he could not be connected with these and would not be in danger of having his ears cut off for taking heed of what the government wanted of him, or having his lips mutilated for what he had told.

His cousin gave him blankets. He slept in a hut with her father. The deaf old man was aware neither that he had come nor was leaving so early that last night's moon, the size of the bicycle's reflector, was still shiny in the sky. The bicycle rode up on spring-hares without disturbing them, in the forest; there was a stink of jackal-fouling still sharp on the dew. Smoke already marked his village; early cooking fires were lit. Then he saw that the smoke, the black particles spindling at his face, were not from cooking fires. Instead of going faster as he pumped his feet against the weight of sand the bicycle seemed to slow along with his mind, to find in each revolution of its wheels the countersurge: to stop; not go on. But there was no way not to reach what he found. The planes only children bothered to look up at any longer had come in the night and dropped something terrible and alive that no one could have read or heard about enough to be sufficiently afraid of. He saw first a bloody kaross, a dog caught on the roots of an upturned tree. The earth under the village seemed to have burst open and flung away what it carried: the huts, pots, gourds, blankets, the tin trunks, alarm-clocks, curtain-booth photographs, bicycles, radios and shoes brought back frcm the mines, the bright cloths young wives wound on their heads, the pretty pictures of white lambs and pink children a* the knees of the golden-haired Christ the Scottish Mission Board first brought long ago—all five generations of the clan's life that had been chronicled by each succeeding generation in episodes told to the next. The huts had staved in like broken anthills. Within earth walls baked and streaked by fire the thatch and roof-poles were ash. He bellowed and stumbled from hut to hut, nothing answered frenzy, not even a chicken rose from under his feet. The walls of his house still stood. It was gutted and the roof had buckled. A black stiff creature lay roasted on its chain in the yard. In one of the huts he saw a human shape transformed the same way, a thing of stiff tar daubed on a recognizable framework. It was the hut where the mad woman lived; when those who had survived fled, they had forgotten her.

The chief's mother and his youngest wife were not among them. But the baby boy lived, and will grow up in the care of the older wives. No one can say what it was the white soldier said over the telephone to his commanding officer, and if the commanding officer had told him what was going to be done, or whether the white soldier knew, as a matter of procedure laid down in his military training for this kind of war, what would be done. The chief hanged himself in the mopane. The police or the army (much the same these days, people confuse them) found the bicycle beneath his dangling shoes. So the family hanger-on still rides it; it would have been lost if it had been safe in the kitchen when the raid came. No one knows where the chief found a rope, in the ruins of his village.

The people are beginning to go back. The dead are properly buried in ancestral places in the mopane forest. The women are to be seen carrying tins and grain panniers of mud up from the river. In talkative bands they squat and smear, raising the huts again. They bring sheaves of reeds exceeding their own height, balanced like the cross-stroke of a majuscular T on their heads. The men's voices sound through the mopane as they choose and fell trees for the roof supports.

A white flag on a mopane pole hangs outside the house whose white walls, built like a white man's, stand from before this time.